ID0594082

THE HEIRS OF COLUMBUS

THE HEIRS

OF COLUMBUS

GERALD

VIZENOR

813.54
V 864

Wesleyan University Press
Published by University Press of New England
Hanover and London

Alverno College
Library Media Center
Milwaukee, Wisconsin

Wesleyan University Press
Published by University Press of New England, Hanover, NH 03755

©1991 by Gerald Vizenor
All rights reserved
Printed in the United States of America   5   4   3   2   1
CIP data appear at the end of the book

The characters, scenes, stories, and construed histories in this novel arise from
imagination; any resemblance to actual persons or events is coincidental.

We are no longer with those who want to possess the world, but with those who want to change it, and it is to the very plan of changing it that it reveals the secrets of its being . . .

The most beautiful book in the world will not save a child from pain; one does not redeem evil, one fights it; the most beautiful book in the world redeems itself; it also redeems the artist. But not the man. Any more than the man redeems the artist. We want the man and the artist to work their salvation together, we want the work to be at the same time an act; we want it to be explicitly conceived as a weapon in the struggle that men wage against evil.

—Jean-Paul Sartre, *"What is Literature?"*

CONTENTS

PART ONE

BLUE MOCCASINS

SANTA MARIA CASINO

Christopher Columbus saw a blue light in the west, but "it was such an uncertain thing," he wrote in his journal to the crown, "that I did not feel it was adequate proof of land." That light was a torch raised by the silent hand talkers, a summons to the New World. Since then, the explorer has become a trickster healer in the stories told by his tribal heirs at the headwaters of the great river.

The Admiral of the Ocean Sea, confirmed in the name of the curia and the crown, was an obscure crossblood who bore the tribal signature of survivance and ascended the culture of death in the Old World. He landed at dawn with no missionaries or naturalists and heard the thunder of shamans in the coral and the stone. "No sooner had we concluded the formalities of taking possession of the island than people began to come to the beach," he wrote in his journal on October 12, 1492, at Samana Cay.

Columbus unfurled the royal banner, and the green cross of the crown shivered on the wind over the island the tribe had named *Guanahaní*. He was blinded by the white sand, the broken sun on the water. He showed his sword to a painted servant on the beach, "and through ignorance he grabbed it by the blade and cut himself."

"In order to win their friendship, since I knew they were a people to be converted and won to our holy faith by love and friendship rather than by force, I gave some of them red caps and glass beads which they hung around their necks," he wrote about his first encounter with tribal people in the New World. "They ought to make good and skilled servants, for they repeat very quickly whatever we say to them," but he misconstrued a tribal pose and later traced his soul to the stories in their blood. "They all go naked as their mothers bore them, including the women, although I saw only one very young girl."

At Samana Cay the great adventurer was touched by a hand talker, a silent tribal wanderer, who wore a golden braid in her hair and carried two wooden puppets. That night she danced with the blue puppets on the sterncastle. The *Santa María* was brushed with a blue radiance.

Columbus and the sailors were haunted by the wild puppets and roused by a golden shimmer on the night water. Samana was an island in the ocean sea that would be imagined but never possessed in the culture of death. Five centuries later the crossblood descendants of the explorer and the hand talker declared a new tribal nation.

"Samana swam out to touch the man from heaven that first night in our New World and here we are on radio," said Stone Columbus.

Columbus was a seasonal voice on late night talk radio because of his surname and the curious stories he told about his inheritance. "She was a natural healer, a tribal hand talker, blessed with silence, and she discovered the incredible truth that the great explorer was tribal and he carried our stories in his blood."

The Heirs of Christopher Columbus are serious over their names and resurrections; the heirs come together at the stone tavern each autumn to remember the best stories about their strain and estate, and the genetic signature that would heal the obvious blunders in the natural world.

The stone tavern, that wondrous circle of warm trickster stones, has been located for more than a hundred generations on a wild blue meadow near the headwaters of the Mississippi River.

The Anishinaabe, the woodland tribe that founded this obscure tavern, the oldest in the New World, remember that Naanabozho, the compassionate tribal trickster who created the earth, had a brother who was a stone: a bear stone, a human stone, a shaman stone, a stone, a stone, a stone.

Naanabozho was the first human born in the world, and the second born, his brother, was a stone. The trickster created the new earth with wet sand. He stood on his toes as high as he could imagine, but the water rose closer to his nose and mouth. He could dream without a mouth or nose, but he would never leave the world to the evil gambler and his dark water. The demons in the water caused him to defecate, and with pleasure, but his shit would not leave; several turds floated near his mouth and nose.

Naanabozho was at the highest point on the earth and could not move, so he invented meditation with trickster stories and liberated his mind over his own excrement. The trickster created this New World with the sand a muskrat held in her paws.

The Heirs of Christopher Columbus created one more New World in their stories and overturned the tribal prophecies that their avian time would end with the arrival of the white man. The heirs warm the stones at the tavern with their stories in the blood. The tavern is on the natural rise of a meadow, and tribal panic holes are sown near the mount. The House of Life is on the descent to the headwaters, the burial ground for the lost and lonesome bones that were liberated by the heirs from museums.

The stones create a natural theater, an uncovered mount that is never touched by storms, curses, and disease; in the winter the stones near the headwaters are a haven for birds, animals, humans, and trickster stories of liberation.

Stone Columbus heard the summer in the spring once more on the occasion of his third resurrection. That season the rush of aspen touched him as a child on his first return from a furnace in a government school; he came back a second time in the arms of the notorious ice woman, and then he drowned in his bingo caravel and heard the push of bears. None of these stories would be true if he had not inherited an unwonted surname and the signature of survivance from the Admiral of the Ocean Sea.

The Heirs of Columbus celebrated the quintessence of their inheritance that season; a blue radiance warmed the tavern stones. The heirs told their stories about creation, the bear codex and hand talkers, the ice woman and moccasin games, panic hole tricksters and saints, the bingo caravel, and the third death and resurrection of the sovereign mariner Stone Columbus.

Christopher Columbus appeared in the dreams of the heirs; the stories that were told at the headwaters were bounden ceremonies, remembrance in the blood, because the bear codex, the last record of their signature of survivance, their blood histories, had been lost at sea. No others on the reservation were visited in dreams or stories by the great explorer; rather, those who revealed their dreams in his name were shunned at first. Later, when the caravels turned a fortune on sovereign bingo, the heirs were embraced as the cash would flow.

Stone Columbus was heartened by his esoteric genetic signature and the stories in his blood; he was a crossblood and his spiritual distance from the tribe seemed to be as natural as the reasons his namesake lost gold, gods, and glories, in the radiance of a hand talker. To be sure, the personal miseries and public troubles with white men over the centuries were blamed on the visions of the crossblood shamans and the estranged stories the heirs told at the stone tavern. The heirs were burdened with the withering ironies of those who had never beheld resurrections in their stories.

The *Santa María Casino*, the decorated bingo flagship, was anchored on the international border near Big Island in Lake of the Woods. The casino was an enormous barge that had been decked for games of chance on the ocean seas of the woodland. The *Niña*, a restaurant, and the *Pinta*, a tax free market, were simulated caravels anchored and moored on the border near the casino.

The *Santa María* was christened and launched as soon as the ice broke in the spring. Stone built a wide cantilevered sterncastle and a cabin that overlooked the spacious casino; on one level he heard the seasons on the lake, and on the lower level he watched the players in the lounge. The two caravels were fitted and christened by early summer in time for the tourists and their search for gold and tribal adventures.

The Fourth of July that year was not a celebration of tribal liberation or independence. Stone was arrested at dawn and detained on warrants that charged him with violations of state tax and gambling laws; the flagship and the caravels were confiscated and towed to a public dock. The next morning, however, a federal judge reversed the state court order; she agreed to review the issues of tribal sovereignty. Our tribal mariner of chance was back on the ocean sea, anchored once more to his stories at the border.

In the first two summers on the water he made a fortune on games and waited for the court to rule on his right to operate a casino as a new reservation moored to an anchor as long as the waters flow in the New World. Border patrols from both countries circled the "dirty mary," copied boat and airplane numbers, estimated the tax free cash flow, and anticipated the court decision that would sink the savage *Santa María Casino*.

Beatrice Lord, the federal judge, ruled in favor of the unusual casino and sanctioned the reservation on an anchor; she so admired the imagination and certitude of the founder that she announced the court decision from the wild sterncastle of the *Santa María Casino* on Columbus Day.

"The federal court finds in favor of Stone Columbus," the judge said over a loudspeaker. Thousands of people in canoes, pontoon boats, and launches heard the voice of the court waver over the water. "The notion of tribal sovereignty is not confiscable, or earth bound; sovereignty is neither fence nor feathers. The essence of sovereignty is imaginative, an original tribal trope, communal and spiritual, an idea that is more than metes and bounds in treaties." The court vacated the claims of the state and ruled that an anchor and caravel is as much a tribal connection to sovereignty as a homestead, mineral rights, the sacred cedar, and the nest of a bald eagle.

"The *Santa María* and the other caravels are limited sovereign states at sea, the first maritime reservations in international waters," the judge announced. "Moreover, the defendant was wise to drop his anchors on the border, knowing, as he must, that future appeals and other remedies could reach the International Court of Justice at The Hague."

The sovereign casino was a natural sensation that summer. Network television reported on the court decision, "the tribe that was lost no more," and pursued the genetic theories of the crossblood founder of the "new casino tribe" who traced his descent to the great adventurer Christopher Columbus.

Stone was pleased to pose on television with Felipa Flowers, the trickster poacher who repatriates tribal remains and sacred pouches from museums, and Miigis, their luminous child, but he would never speak to a camera; however, he was eager to be heard on national talk show radio. Felipa, Miigis, Stone, and Admire, the mongrel with the blue tongue, lived on the *Santa María Casino*. The mongrel was a healer, she whistled and barked on radio, but she shied at television cameras.

"Radio is real, television is not," he reminded the radio listeners. His grandparents listened to talk radio late at night on the reservation; the bold lies and arguments over the truth that he heard as a child hurried his sense of adventure, imagination, and the stories in his blood.

Stone was heard by millions of people late at night on talk radio that wild summer. The crossblood of the northern air told his stories about the stone tavern, his resurrections, and the genetic signature of the heirs that would heal the nation. He spoke from the sterncastle of his casino; a flotilla of canoes, powerboats, and floatplanes from the cities circled the *Santa María*. The gamblers were white, most of them were on vacation, urban adventurers who would lose at bingo and slot machines with pleasure on a moored reservation.

"Admiral Luckie White is on the air. . ."

"Stone Columbus is here as usual, and who you hear is what you see," he said that summer night from the sterncastle of the *Santa María Casino*.

"Admiral Luckie White is on the air, your late night host and voice of the night on Carp Radio." The radio was heard in four directions from enormous loudspeakers on the masts of the casino and the caravels. "Columbus is back to answer your questions and mine tonight. Here we go once more with the truth in the dark, so, how do you expect our listeners to buy the stories that your brother is a stone, a common rock?"

"Stone is my name, not my brother, and we are not common," said Stone Columbus. His voice was a primal sound that boomed over the black water. "The stone is my totem, my stories are stones, there are tribal stones, and the brother of the first trickster who created the earth was a stone, stone, stone."

"Really, but how can you be a stone, a real stone, and be talking on radio?" she asked, and then paused for a commercial. The talks from the casino two or three times a week had attracted new listeners and many eager advertisers. Carp Radio had discovered a new world on the *Santa María Casino*.

"Stones hold our tribal words and the past in silence, in the same way that we listen to stories in the blood and hold our past in memories," he said, and waved to several people boarding the caravel.

"Stone, listen, our listeners know you were born on a reservation, and we understand how proud you are to be an Indian, so how can you claim to be a direct descendant of a stone and Christopher Columbus?"

"Columbus was Mayan," said Stone.

"You must be stoned," she said, and laughed on the air. Her voice bounced on the water, and the boats rocked with laughter near the casino. Admire barked at the boats and healed the night. "Really, you must be stoned on that reservation boat, Columbus was Italian, not a Mayan Indian."

"The Maya brought civilization to the savages of the Old World and the rest is natural," said Stone. "Columbus escaped from the culture of death and carried our tribal genes back to the New World, back to the great river, he was an adventurer in our blood and he returned to his homeland."

"His homeland, now wait a minute, this is serious radio."

"My stories are evermore serious, serious, serious," he said and teased the sounds of the words. Admire whistled a tune from a

9

familiar symphony based on tribal themes. Felipa laughed and inserted a tape cassette in the recorder and played the *New World Symphony*, by Antonín Dvořák.

Stone posed with Miigis that night as an orchestra leader on the sterncastle of the *Santa María Casino*. The mast was decorated with spirit catchers that held the wild beads of light from the boats on the lake. Felipa touched them from behind, the wondrous trickster on the ocean sea in a scarlet tunic, and her daughter in a blue robe. Admire heard her own bark echo on the loudspeaker; she bounced in a circle on the deck of the casino.

"Mayan genes, give me a break," said Admiral White.

"The truth is in our genes," said Stone.

"Right, we are what our genes must pretend."

"We are the tribal heirs of the great explorer," said Stone.

"What are you playing?"

"The *Santa María Overture*," said Stone.

"No, that's Dvořák," said Luckie White.

"Dvořák was at the headwaters," said Stone.

"Please, tell our listeners why."

"Dvořák heard tribal music in the stones," said Stone.

"What about Columbus?"

"He sought gold and tribal women," said Stone.

"So, what did he find?"

"He found his homeland at the headwaters."

"Really, so what's the real story?"

"Samana, the golden healer," said Stone.

"The truth at last, but first a commercial announcement from those wise companies that buy our time and make the truth possible in the dark," said Admiral White.

"Samana is our hand talker, the golden woman of the ocean seas and sister to the fish, and she touched his soul and set the wounded adventurer free on October 28, 1492, at Bahia de Bariay in Oriente Province, Cuba," he said, and smiled over the dates and names.

Felipa danced on the deck that warm night; she was touched by the memories of his stories, the sound of his creation. She could hear the end of the culture of death on the sterncastle of the casino,

10

and she sensed the last of the heartsore stories of a broken civilization.

"Stone, wait a minute, you leap from stones, to genes, to goldfish, to dates and places, and back again, so take your time now and spell it out in your own words to our listeners," said Admiral White.

"October 29, 1492, at Rio de la Luna."

"You changed the date."

"Columbus is ever on the move in our stories," said Stone.

"This is a good time for a commercial."

Stone connected the tape recorder to the loudspeakers and turned the volume higher with the allegro con fuoco of the *New World* Symphony. The moon was a wicked sliver in the west; on the water the moon was shredded on the breeze. Felipa undressed and dove into the black water. Stone dove into her wake and swam at her side to the island. They made love on a granite boulder; the mosquitos sounded louder in their heat. They heard the bears, the breath of bears, and warm paws on the stone. Later, a cool wind touched them; the ice woman lived in a cave on the other side of the island.

"The ice woman saved me once," he said on the granite. Stone touched her breasts and moved closer to the heat of her thighs. "I crashed through the thin ice, the paper ice that teased me to rush in the spring, and sank deeper and deeper in the cold clear water. I could see the hole in the ice above me, and the veins on the underside of the ice, but my arms were numbed, my vision blurred, and the last breath of cold water was ecstatic. The ice woman brought me back, and that was my second resurrection."

The *Santa María Casino* paid high stakes to hundreds of winners and earned millions besides, and the tax free market caravel was a second gold mine. Stone earned more than a million dollars a season, and there were four summers in the name of the great explorer. Even the restaurant caravel turned a profit on pretentious bad taste, a commodities menu of fry bread, oatmeal, macaroni, and glorified wild rice.

Stone Columbus was the proud mariner on a moored reservation, a trickster creation on an ocean sea in the new tribal world.

11

He heard the seasons turn from the wild sterncastle of the *Santa María Casino*. Summer touched the spring, and he discovered gold in the name of his blood and survivance. He heard the blue puppets dance on the decks, and then, late one night in a thunderstorm, at the crowning point of his casino glories and stories, the casino and the caravels were cracked by lightning.

Felipa and Miigis were on shore and survived the storm. The few gamblers in the casino were able to abandon the reservation and rode the storm in their own boats. The spirit catchers on the mast burned, and the blue medicine poles were overturned and crashed into the casino; the cantilevered sterncastle burst at the seams. Admire, a blue light in the water, was rescued by a woman in a powerboat.

The *Santa María* lost her anchor and moorings as a sovereign casino; she bashed on a granite reef, the beam groaned and the flagship sank near the island, the sudden end of a new reservation. The great trickster explorer discovered gold and then drowned in his scarlet tunic; he washed ashore a rich man with thousands of bingo cards.

Stone was broken and lost on the cold granite; his black hair was mussed with weeds and wild tinsel. The bears pushed the seasons down to the shore at dawn and pawed the remains of the casino and the caravels; the spirit catchers, macaroni, and polyurethane were lost on the woodland sea in the last thunderstorm of the season.

Samana, the crossblood black bear and lonesome hand talker on the island, hauled the mariner to a granite boulder. She teased his ears with her nose and blew on his eyes and mouth; when she blew harder the other bears danced on the mount near shore. Samana was a shaman, as her mother was a bear, and her touch would heal the heir with stories in the blood. Stone heard the wild dance of blue puppets on the stones.

Samana touched his head and the bears pushed him back from death with a blue radiance; the stones were warmed on the shore and held his graven image. He was a hand talker in the maw of the bear. She was his heart and memories; she teased his third resurrection in the stone.

STONE TAVERN

Truman Columbus shouts that the "dikinaagan of civilization is located at the headwaters of the gichiziibi," or the cradle board of civilization is at the Mississippi River. "Civilization started right here in our stories at the river we named the gichiziibi," she shouted that night with her back to the warm stones in the tavern on the mount.

The sun was low and the last leaves on the autumn birch were undone on the blue wind from the mountains. The stone tavern is laid on a mount at the rise of a natural meadow. Red pine reach in the west, birch run lower with the river. The first stones were tricksters at the wild creation of the tribe and the earth. The stones once told stories, trickster stories; now the stones listen at the mount. The stones heal and remember the blue radiance of creation and resurrections. The stones hold the beat of water drums, and the chatter of blue puppets, both common sounds to the Heirs of Christopher Columbus.

Three stones have been stolen since the creation of the tavern. Each time those who were near the stolen trickster stones lost their vision, withered, and died in a few months time. The first stone was stolen by a missionary; the members of his parish touched the stone and were blinded. That stone was thrown into the ocean sea

13

and never recovered. The second stone was stolen by an anthropologist who held the trickster in a display case at the university; the minds of students withered before the anthropologist died and the stone was returned. The third stone, a warm round healer, was stolen and broken by a blond shaman; she sold hundreds of trickster slivers to ostentatious head healers in California.

The number of heirs is a tribal secret, but there were nine who told stories that autumn evening at the stone tavern: Truman Columbus, the shouter, and her spouse with the same names; Binn Columbus and her son Stone; Memphis, the black panther; Gracioso Browne, the panic hole historian; Felipa Flowers, the gorgeous trickster poacher; Caliban, the great white mongrel; Samana, the shaman bear from Big Island in Lake of the Woods. Miigis, the luminous child, and Admire, the healer who whistled with a blue tongue, were there with Stone and Felipa.

"We are created in stories, the same stories that hold our memories and thousands of generations in these stones," shouted Truman. She invited a blond anthropologist to hear their stories at the tavern. The blonde promised to be silent; she was interested in bioshamanism and resurrections.

"We remember our stories in the blood each autumn at the tavern and mine are on resurrection," she said to the blonde. Truman shouts at stones to summon memories. She learned to shout as a child, practiced as a lover and mother; however, she was slow to learn silence in the best stories. She hears stories in the blood and then she shouts them into the world.

"Stone is my grandson and we inherited the same signature from the great explorer, but no one else on the reservation has been resurrected three times," she shouted, and then paused to brush the stones and hear the silence. "He died the first time in a thunderstorm at the reservation school." The others remembered the government school in silence; the tavern stories were not a competition for popular memories, but a remembrance in the blood.

"The teachers rushed the children to the coal bin," she continued to shout. "Stone, as usual, never followed instructions and climbed into the giant ventilators when the other children were removed to the dark basement.

"The wind wailed as the wind does on the reservation, as the wind does in the white pine," she shouted, and then wailed to hear the wind; the others wailed in turn, but the blond anthropologist remained silent. "Stone heard the wild demons in the mouth of the cold air return, and the same demons came to me in a dream at the mission. That boy mocked the sounds of the storm for no good reason but fear, and then he was gone, vanished in the ventilator.

"A sudden burst of wind sucked two children, books, blue papers, erasures, into that giant, even the Stars and Stripes. Everything near the metal ventilators shot from the classroom to the black furnace in the basement. The children and the flag were dead, covered with dust and coal soot.

"The storm was real and the furnace came to me in a dream," she strained to whisper. The anthropologist leaned closer to listen; blond hair shrouded her narrow face. Truman moved her hands over her head as she remembered the resurrection on the furnace mount. "Stone and the other child were laid out on the cold concrete.

"I touched them both, and blew on them, but the other child would not hold me in his dreams," she shouted and turned toward her grandson and the warm stones. "That sweet child never returned to my hands, he would not come to me in dreams, he never heard our stories in the blood.

"Stone heard the bear in his blood, he dreamed he was a bear at his own death, and then he came back to the headwaters," she shouted, and turned to the panther on the other side of the tavern. "He listened to the wind, the rush of aspen, and laughed at the blue light in the basement."

Truman raised her hands and trained a great bear shadow over the stones, over the meadow to the headwaters of the river; the shadow stood with the red pine west of the tavern; the bear shadow was lost in the last burst of sun over the horizon. The mongrel moaned, the panther purred, and the other heirs leaned on the warm stones in the circle.

Memphis, the black panther who was liberated by the heirs from a game park, remembered the bears and trickster creation stories at the tavern. She saw the blue radiance of creation in the stone and the blood of the heirs. "We imagined each other out there in the beginning," she said to the mongrel Caliban. "Panther and brother, cedar and bear, we were the same stones, the same blue heat, and we imagined who we would be, stone or panther, someone warm in the world."

Memphis raised one paw and leaned closer in the circle. She waited to hear the last crows overhead and then continued to push the stories into the night. "When imagination dies we become lonesome slaves to our bodies, prisoners to our sounds, species, and culture. The stories of the panther are my best memories, but what you hear is not what you might see in me."

Caliban, the great white reservation mongrel and heir to the stone, remembered the same stories of imagination as the panther and the shaman bear. "Once upon a time the mongrels were the stories of creation, we dreamed humans into being and then out to the sea in search of their own stories in the blood, but humans lost their humor over land, gold, slaves, and time.

"Mongrels created the best humans, we had that crossblood wild bounce in our blood, but we never imagined that on two feet the beasts would lose their humor and memories, and turn against those who hauled them from the muck," said the mongrel. Caliban turned to the warm stones and panted; he smiled at the bear and the panther and the other heirs in the circle. He admired the mongrel with the blue tongue.

"Let sleeping dogs lie," said Truman Columbus. He boasted that he was the patron saint of crossbloods on the reservation; hundreds of mongrels, even the head campers from the universities, responded to his coarse manner and the croak of his voice. The saint had a nose for tribal turnovers and once lived on stories and his nicknames from season to season until he married and assumed the names of his spouse. "My friends are worth their weight in gold," he said, and pointed to the mongrels who trailed him to the headwaters. None but the heirs dared to enter the stone tavern. Truman croaked that the mongrels were his heirs, but not heirs to the stories in the blood. "Caliban is the one mongrel who bears the beat of the stone and the signature of the Heirs of Christopher Columbus."

Stone is the richest crossblood on the reservation, water or land, and he is remembered, if for no other reason, because his maternal grandparents have the same names; he teases his own stories with imitations of their shouts and croaks. From time to time he brushes the stones in silence.

Stone wears a blue mask with golden eyes and ears at the stone tavern on the mount; the blue metal was peened thin with a high forehead and an aquiline nose, the image of his survivance and namesake of the Admiral of the Ocean Sea.

"Every dog has his day," said Memphis.

"Mongrels have their humans," said Caliban.

"Old dog, new tricks," croaked Truman.

"The trickster remembers that we created humans," said Caliban. "So, what happened is that the crossbloods were cornered by the pretenders and that was the end of humor in the blood." The panther purred and cleaned her paws. The moon leaned over the birch and pine east of the headwaters and the House of Life.

"A dog's life," said Memphis.

"Once upon a time the panthers and the bears were wiser than they are now," said Caliban. "They held their distance and ended up as trophies, but the mongrels stayed closer to the campfires and imagined humans on the run with two legs."

Samana, the radiant bear shaman and heir to the genetic signature, turned low to the mongrel in the tavern; she raised her arms to speak, and the moon flashed in the black hair on her arms and hands. Samana has talked with her hands since the death of her father; her mother was a bear, and her father was the last shaman on the island who talked wild with bears and tamed thunderstorms. "Blue puppets in the manger," she said with her hands.

17

Caliban insisted that the others hear his stories on imagination, the seven memories held at the stone tavern by the Heirs of Columbus. "Once there was a crossblood who wrote about the mongrels that we inspired," he said, and then waited to hear the mongrels bark outside the tavern. "We imagined the author, gave him the names, the mongrel healers and tricksters in his stories.

"Pure Gumption, we inspired the human to write, was a shaman mongrel who glowed and healed with her paws and tongue. She attended a priest, pawed the lonesome, licked the sick back to health. She liberated and healed the animals and birds that were held in humans, silent prisoners in bone and blood," said Caliban.

"Pure Gumption was a shiner, blue radiance in his stories, but when we presented a collection of our stories, by a shaman mongrel, the publishers were evasive and stood behind their two legs," he said. "We created humans, put them on two legs to slow them down, and then they pretend their blood and bone is the survival of the best."

Stone remembered the tails that the hand talkers wore to tease the demons; he wore their tail to tease his stories from the stone, and to bait the anthropologist. The tails are woven with cattails and willow and decorated with red leaves. He turned his tail on the stones. The panther purred and the tails turned blue on the stone. "Imagine our silence in the stone," he said, and moved the border to bait the mongrels outside. "The hand talkers are from the primal tribes, the silent people, the great wanderers from other worlds."

"They lost their ears to the tricksters at a moccasin game," said the panic hole historian Gracioso Browne. "The hand talkers touched a bad moccasin and were released from the sound of the world."

Stone must remember his stories with comments from the other heirs. Gracioso, for instance, believes that "seasonal resurrections create new stories in the blood, stories that honor new memories, a new inheritance."

"The hand talkers show their stories in the summer, in silence, and leave their handprints around the world," said Stone. Miigis laid her hands on the warm stones, Admire at her side; she whistled

18

a tune from the *New World* Symphony. "The water demons hear no stories in the summer." The hand talkers wander from many tribes and threaten no one with their silence; their hands remember the culture of death and civilization in two worlds.

"There are black hand talkers, and white shakers, and they pack their words in little boxes," said his mother, Binn Columbus. "Those little boxes hold the shouts and laughter of the hand talkers, and their loneliness, and the boxes are mine to remember." She learned as a child to hear the voices of shadows.

Binn lives with her boxes, three men, and eighteen children in a cabin buried in the woods near the headwaters. The stones and trees reveal their memories and the secrets of the tribes; she listened to trees, water, and containers. The water mentions the weather, and the boxes hold the best secrets. She hears treasures in cardboard and secrets in cedar chests; she hears words in piano benches, closets, even in pockets. "The most lonesome voices come from the pouches carried by the hand talkers."

Stone once sent his mother cigar boxes to hear his stories from the *Santa María Casino*. She hears stories in the blood, secrets of the heart and bone, from most containers, even the abandoned bodies of automobiles. Binn remembers marvelous stories from common trash on the reservation.

"Christopher Columbus, you remember, was enchanted by a golden hand talker on his first voyage to the New World," said Stone. "Samana was a silent healer, she touched the great adventurer and his spirit landed here on the stones at the headwaters."

"Touch me, heal me in a panic hole," chanted Gracioso.

"Columbus was a bad shadow, tired and broken, because he lost most of his body parts on the way, so the old shamans heated some stones and put him back together again," croaked Truman. "Harm, the water shaman, said he dreamed a new belly for the explorer, and Shin, the bone shaman, called in a new leg from the underworld, and he got an eye from the sparrow woman, so you might say that we created this great explorer from our own stones at the tavern."

"Columbus has been seen, almost whole, at the stone tavern for five hundred years," said Stone. "Samana touched his soul and lured his spirit to the headwaters, and here we are, the tribal heirs to that primal union."

"Columbus lives in a silver box," said Binn.

"Touch me, heal me in a panic hole," chanted Gracioso.

"The Maya created Columbus," said Stone. "The dreams that carried him back to his stories in the blood are the same dreams that heal, he is the bear signature of our humor and survival."

"Panthers and our imagination rise in his name," said Memphis.

"Civilization ends in my name," said Caliban.

"Columbus discovered dogs that never barked," said Binn.

"The Maya created tobacco and civilization," croaked Truman. "Now we got computers and fast food, so the old cultures must come to an end in warm, reasonable sentences." The mongrels bark outside the stone tavern when the old man croaks. "We got the names down, the causes are beaten by chance, and the last surprise is that sudden decadence of imagination."

Truman removed his blue moccasins and summoned the heirs to choose their sides in a moccasin game as he remembered the stories in the blood. "The game that saved the heirs from the water demons," he croaked. Binn, Caliban, and Gracioso moved to his side of the stone circle.

Truman removed her blue moccasins and summoned Stone, Memphis, Felipa, and Samana to her side of the game. "The natural balance of blue moccasins," she shouted. Miigis, Admire, and the anthropologist watched the game, one on each side of the moccasins.

Truman turned four copper coins under each of the moccasins. The coins were polished, one bears the image of the great explorer and their namesake. The game opened in his stories on the last game with the wiindigoo, the evil cannibal, on one side, and the ice woman with the tribe on the other side. The moccasin game in the stone tavern that autumn became the same game in his stories.

The wiindigoo leans over a stone on one side of the moccasins. The tribal dreamers and the animals are on the other side; the mongrels nose the old moccasins. The players beat their drums, a slow beat at the start of the game of choice; to win, the tribe must touch the moccasin that covers the marked coin.

"Choose your players for the last great moccasin game of the tribe," said the wiindigoo. He is clean and handsome, a deceptive water demon; the sound of love flutes surround him at the game. Tribal women are drawn to his blond hair and his perfect smile; his hesitation at first touch is the lure that leads to death. The last touch is evil; the flutes would turn to moans, breath to bone rattles, and the handsome man would become a skeleton. No one has ever beat the wiindigoo in a moccasin game.

"Play with me to save your children from the water demons," said the wiindigoo. The children taunted the blond demon with bear paws and their best wooden masks; one pretended to be the ice woman, others were bears and the wind.

The wiindigoo turned the four copper coins in one hand, and then placed one under each moccasin. The mongrels barked at the demon; he smiled and thunder sounded in the distance.

The tribal players beat their drums, the shamans meditated on the marked coin under one of the moccasins, and the water demon countered their choice with a moan. The tribe lost the first and second rounds of the game. One round remained, the last chance to save their children from the demon.

"The tribe is a game, the children are a game, but evil and fear are chances, and nothing in the world is more real than the moccasin game," said the wiindigoo. "This is your last chance to save the game and the real."

The tribal players were distracted with fear and pleaded with the ice woman to leave her cold cave on the island and win the moccasin game in their name. She is a hand talker, an ancient silent woman who has been blamed for the death of thousands of men in winter, those who were lost in storms. Children mock her frozen motion, and now the tribe wants her to save their culture with a breath of winter in the summer.

The wiindigoo turned the coins, the last round of the moccasin game. He smiled once more and, as the children had done, he moved his hands to mock the ice woman and the hand talkers at the circle. The demon had no sense of pain or weather, he could not sense the seasons, but the others shiver near the game; that winter in the summer was their last chance to survive the moccasin game.

The ice woman leaned closer to the wiindigoo and blew on his hands as he reached to touch a moccasin; the circle turned colder and colder. Frost covered the moccasins, and the blond demon stiffened over the game; he reached once more, and evil was frozen solid with a smile. He would have won the last round if he had turned the moccasin; the coin with the image of the explorer was there, at the end of his frozen hand. The sonnies danced around the ice woman; she was too cold to touch, but the children touched each other and pretended to be cold and adorable.

"Too much winter in the heart," shouted Truman.

"Feed that frozen demon to the mongrels," said Caliban.

"Never, the mongrels would become water demons and that would be the end of the game and our stories," croaked Truman. The mongrels barked at the sound of his stories. "The ice woman carried the frozen wiindigoo back to her cave where he remains to this day with one hand out, the ice demon waiting for a thaw and his chance to win the moccasin game."

"Winter, be mine in a panic hole," said Gracioso.

"His summer is our end," said the bear shaman with her blue hands. Samana has lived on the same island as the ice woman for more than a century. She said the bears praise the winter and honor the ice woman in the summer, and the heirs must do the same to endure.

The ice woman holds the wiindigoo, the four blue moccasins, and the copper coins at the back of her cave. Once each summer she turns the coins and thaws the moccasins, a tribute to the four seasons and the memories of tribal chance.

Gracioso Browne was bound so tight with erotic memories and time that his stories in the blood are closer to sound bites, shadows and measures. He was educated in business and economics, wears a black suit and two wrist watches, and records animals on a portable video camera. The mongrels learned to cock their heads and pose, and then bark with pleasure at their human images on screen.

Gracioso hounded his miniature soul to bear the burdens of time and loneliness in the cities. The denouement downtown was the same each month; a video recording of his shouts over panic holes on the reservation. The meadows near the headwaters were in bloom with the natural shouts of the heirs and crossbloods.

"The old men, cheated out of their land, became tricksters, and some shouted into panic holes," said Gracioso. He leaned over to demonstrate the rich sound of a tribal shout, but there were no panic holes in the stone tavern, so his shout was inhibited, faint, a panic mime. Outside, the mongrels heard the trace and barked into their holes. Admire moaned, and the blonde bounced with silent humor.

"My shouts are thunder, my storms return to the earth, a sound that restores the natural balance," he boasted. "The meadows hear my thunder, and the flowers grow, the earth loves to hear me shout.

"The Baron of Patronia, a distant great uncle who became a nobleman in a land allotment hoax, was the original shouter on his reservation. Luster Browne, as he was known to the tribe, meditated with shouts over panic holes, and he became a gardener by chance because flowers bloomed on the beds and meadows that heard his shouts.

"The California Transportation Department paid him a tribal ransom to shout over the weeds on the highway medians, and sure enough the wild flowers bloomed the next morning at seventeen minutes before eleven," said Gracioso.

"Must we know the time?" asked Felipa Flowers.

"Pacific Standard Time," he responded. Gracioso touches both of his watches when he smiles, and he smiles between sentences. He was a miniature healer in his best stories, and he practiced humor over his own whimsies. "I was there, on time, and recorded the whole thing, and cut the best contracts as his professional panic hole agent."

California invited hundreds of inspired advocates to shout over the oleander, broom, and poppies on the medians, but there were no blooms. Luster was the shaman of the shouts, so his shouts were taped and broadcast over the roads and parks to conserve water. He earned residual fees for the recorded use of his shouts and became the richest man on the reservation until bingo was discovered and ruled sovereign on the *Santa María Casino*.

23

The governor and several state legislators copied the tapes and turned the tribal shouts on their private gardens, a minor scandal that became an oasis movement of the primal shout. Magnolias and wisteria matured in a few seasons; the shaman of shouts heartened new meditation movements in parks, gardens, and over common house plants.

"Luster died over a panic hole on a meadow near the headwaters," said Gracioso. He leaned and shouted once more to honor the memories of the old man and his panic hole meditation. His honor shout was richer and mature. "At seven minutes past five one summer afternoon, at the same moment of his death, his shouts ended on hundreds of tape recordings, the trees and flowers waited but no other shouts would heal them in the cities."

The Minnesota Headwaters Commission and Golden Gate Park in San Francisco erected two bronze statues of the tribal shouter, one in each state, over natural panic holes. The statues are haunted by the spirit of the panic hole shaman. Shouts are heard at night, and the blooms are wild and rich near that statue.

"Everyday there are lonesome people at the panic holes with their sick plants," said Gracioso. "Some of them are deaf, but they wait for the statue to shout and heal their plants, and even the old people are healed."

Felipa Flowers, the trickster poacher, remembered stories in the land of the dead; dreams that she was the last survivor in the tribal world. In the land of the dead she heard no stories, the dead were silent hand talkers. She raised one arm to salute, in the manner of the hand talkers, and lost a hand; she reached to save one hand and lost the other. Her body was broken and piled near a bronze statue and stained glass windows of a church.

Felipa tried to learn the stories of the hand talkers, but she had no hands. She awoke at last, but she was in another dream. Then in the second dream a shaman with a golden mask carved two new hands from a live cedar tree. The wood was cold, bloodless, but the hands moved. She saluted and pleaded with the shaman to push her from the dream and the stories of death.

"You are dead in our dreams to learn the secrets of the bear codex," the shaman with the golden mask said in her second

24

dream. He printed the surname "Le Plongeon" on the back of her wooden hand. When she awakened from both dreams she remembered the name.

More than a decade later, when she was a fashion model, she located the bear codex by chance in a bookshop on Charing Cross Road in London. The codex was handwritten and disguised in a book entitled *Pearls in Shells*, by Augustus Le Plongeon. She saw the name and remembered the dream. The quarto was bound in blue cloth; the name of the author was printed on the cover. She bought the book and discovered later that the bear codex was an incredible revelation from the ancient Maya House of Cocom.

Felipa said the title "Bear Codex" and the date "October 28, 1908" were printed by hand on the title page, but no publisher was indicated. Augustus Le Plongeon died two months later on December 13, 1908, in Brooklyn, New York.

Le Plongeon, she learned later, was an eccentric scholar and dedicated archaeologist who believed that the Maya were the original civilization in the New World. The Maya founded world civilization, and the hand talkers carried the bear signature of survivance, their stories in the blood, to the Old World.

Felipa and the heirs to the stories were convinced that the bear codex was a translation of an original picture codex. Augustus Le Plongeon and his wife, Alice, interviewed a tribal man in Espita, Yucatán, who was one hundred fifty years old at the time; this man said, through a translator, that an even older man had a sacred book "none could read." Augustus decided that the book the old man remembered was the picture codex of the Maya House of Cocom.

The Heirs of Christopher Columbus must remember their stories in the blood each autumn at the stone tavern near the headwaters, because the bear codex was lost in a storm that night on the *Santa María Casino*.

The bear codex revealed that the bear signature of survivance, the inheritance of a nonesuch genetic code, was the measure of civilization and the power of resurrections. These inherited stories in the blood and the picture codex were carried by tribal hand talkers to the Old World and remembered by a hundred tribal generations. There the silent balams, the shaman hand talkers, were honored as the eccentric healers and emissaries of civilization.

Ptolemy ordered that the bear codex be translated, copied on papyrus, and deposited in the Library of Alexandria. Felipa read in *The Vanished Library*, by Luciano Canfora, that the "Ptolemies and their librarians set out not only to collect every book in the world, but to translate them all into Greek." The library was destroyed by fire. The original bear codex and the copies were burned once in the Old World, and once more by conquistadors in the New World. The last translation of the bear codex was lost in a thunderstorm.

The Maya were the first to imagine the universe and to write about their stories in the blood. The shamans, the healers, and the hand talkers with their blue puppets presented a heliocentric cosmos over the geocentered notions at that time in the Old World. The bear codex pictured the sun as the center of the universe, as the spirit is the center of imagination and tribal civilization. These were strange ideas in a culture of death that held the earth as the center; the bear shamans and hand talkers touched an interior vision, and told the Old World how to use the arithmetic naught in measures of time.

"Jesus Christ and Columbus are Maya," said Felipa.

"The Maya were on our time, and we got the same genetic signature from the hand talkers," said Gracioso. "The New World presented the Old World with camels, bioshamans, zero, the touch of civilization, and calendar time, and created the first cultural debt that has never been paid on time."

"So, look at what we got in return," shouted Truman.

"Warm stones and panic holes," said Caliban.

"Ten percent and resurrections," said Stone.

"Closet shamans," said Caliban.

"Jesus returned in a burst of blue radiance," said Felipa.

"His shroud bears our stories," said Stone.

"The Shroud of Turin can be heard at the seams," said Binn.

"Someone should shroud the heirs," croaked Truman.

26

"Fait accompli," said Caliban.

"Who would that be then?" asked Binn.

"The Genome Project and the wiindigoo on ice," said Stone.

"The blonde is entitled to one petition," said Caliban.

"How does that dog whistle?" asked the blond anthropologist.

"The same way she sings," said Stone.

"Admire learned how to whistle just like a human, she puts her blue lips together and blows, and blows, and blows some more," shouted Truman.

The Heirs of Christopher Columbus move with two shadows in a blue radiance at the headwaters. The moon was clear; the hand talkers and tribal spirits danced on the thin ice clouds over the north. Someone old shouted in the distance, shouted over the birch, and the mongrels barked back to be sure; another shout, older, closer, and there were more stories to remember in the blood. The stone tavern on the mount was blue, the night was blue that autumn of the House of Life.

STORM PUPPETS

The Mayan shamans and hand talkers landed unused in the Old World and declared their heritable radiance in the shadows and spiritual causes of Jesus Christ, Christopher Columbus, and Sephardic Jews.

Columbus would survive the culture of death, the wicked histories of his time, the crusades, medieval colophons, burdens of shame, and morose politics of the mind, with an untold radiance. He inherited the signature of survivance and tribal stories in the blood from his mother, and she inherited the genetic signature from maternal ancestors. Women, the bearers of the genetic signature, and their heirs were once active in the spice and parchment trade; the survivors were obscure descendants of the healers and hand talkers from the New World. That blue radiance has been carried in blood and stories by adventurers, traders, mystics, dancers, and puppeteers in the Old World.

Susanna di Fontanarossa was the daughter of a weaver and the bearer of the signature; she was a dancer and a dreamer of wild seasons. Notarial records in the municipal archives reveal that she married Domenico Colombo, a wool carder and weaver. Six years later in the winter she heard the stories in the blood and conceived a son. Cristoforo was newborn and baptized in October 1451 at Genoa.

Cristoforo Colombo heard the Old World stories at the end of the exotic spice trade. He was a child of "seductive aromas" and pain; touched with a radiance, an unrevealed signature of survivance. He would bear the stories in his blood, and a hand talker would bear his child at the headwaters of the great river in the New World.

Columbus was curious and lauded, to be sure; he was embraced and healed by women, and his pose as a religious man endured in the Old World. His letters were decorated with a small cross, and he copied prayers, but he would be remembered as peevish, stubborn, and pompous. His solitude and memories were pained by women; at the same time he was sustained by a regnant woman, and his shadows, the stories in his blood, were liberated by a silent woman on his first voyage to the New World, but his bones were denied the honor and solace of the grave; his remains were denied peace and salvation. He was disembodied at sea and pursued the suck of gold to the last civil encomiums of the crown.

"In his readiness to translate thought into action, in lively curiosity and accurate observation of natural phenomena, in his joyous sense of adventure and desire to win wealth and recognition, he was a modern man," wrote Samuel Eliot Morison in *Admiral of the Ocean Sea*. Columbus was a child of weavers, healers, and the sea in an unstable city; indeed, he would be a modern man, a tragic man, because his stories and blue shadows would abandon the burdens of his bones in the Old World.

Genoa was an ancient free commune that became a rich republic; the wealth of the port city was based on trade. The stories of adventure in the east were told by bold spice traders and remembered by the weavers of cloth; freedom and wealth at that time were associated with precious stones, the aromas and secret origins of cinnamon, ginger, cloves, and other spices.

Columbus was two years old when Muhammad II, the founder of the Ottoman Empire, captured Constantinople and overturned the Byzantine Empire. The stories continued to be told, but the spice trade from the east had ended; the ships would no longer sail from Genoa to the Black Sea.

"Genoa shuddered with the fear of becoming poor from one moment to the next," wrote Gianni Granzotto in *Christopher Columbus*. "The Turkish conquest of Constantinople would bring with it a complete severing of the spice route, which for so long had served as the lifeline of the Mediterranean world's economy and politics and shaped its ways of living and thinking. Everything became unstable, uncertain."

Columbus matured on the natural pitch of the sea and the stories in his blood; he first sailed near the coast to buy wool and to sell the cloth that his father had woven. When he was fourteen he sailed near the western coastline. Later he was aroused and pained by the dance of blue puppets on the island of Corsica in the Ligurian Sea. The wooden puppets chattered, a sound that touched his bones; a sound he would hear at a convent, and a third time on his first voyage to the New World, and once more in a storm at sea. He was haunted by the puppets and the puppeteers; the women were slender and silent, their hands were blue to the wrist. He was told that the hand talkers were Sephardic Jews. The ocean sea was in his bones, and the blue puppets were untold stories in his blood.

"The Admiral was a well built man of more than medium stature, long visaged with cheeks somewhat high, but neither fat nor thin," wrote his son Ferdinand Columbus in *The Life of the Admiral Christopher Columbus*. "He had an aquiline nose and his eyes were light in color; his complexion too was light, but kindling to a vivid red. In youth his hair was blond, but when he came to his thirtieth year it all turned white."

Stone Columbus practiced a dream that he was the captain of a spice ship that sailed into Constantinople when it was the capital of the Byzantine Empire. There, in a paradise of aromas, he encountered blue puppets and erotic women. They were the ancestors of the silent healers who revealed the bear codex of the Maya House of Cocom. Stone was warned by the hand talkers that the curse of a twisted penis had been laid on men as revenge by the women who were burned with the bear codex and other manuscripts at the Library of Alexandria.

30

Christopher Columbus wrote a secret letter at sea, on his return from the first voyage to the New World. The letter was sealed in a container to survive a demonic storm. He announced his discoveries, insecurities, silence and sense of separation, the visions that pursued him on the ocean sea, and his wild pleasures and liberation with a hand talker named Samana. She had "golden breasts and thighs," and she was the "first woman who moved me from the curse of my secret pain," he revealed in the letter.

"So, in his cabin on that pitching and rolling vessel the Admiral got out his vellum, quill, and inkhorn, wrote a brief account of the voyage and of his discoveries, wrapped the parchment in a waxed cloth, ordered it to be headed up in a great wooden barrel, and cast into the sea," wrote Samuel Eliot Morison in *Admiral of the Ocean Sea*.

Columbus was pained by persistent erections; his enormous clubbed penis curved to the right, a disease of fibrous contracture during an erection. He was born with a burdensome penis that once was presented as comic in ancient dramas. The smaller penis was a prick of endearment in some coteries; his was a torturous penis, a curse that turned the mere thought of sexual pleasure to sudden pain.

That his radiance was misunderstood as sexual heat did not ease his torment and agonies, a cruel burden that slackened nowhere but at sea. He could not masturbate or have intercourse without pain, and the hard curve of his penis made intromission even more arduous. He was aroused and pained by the dancers, the hand talkers, even by memories and the chatter of the blue puppets. The discovery of the internal penis would not ease his torment, but he humored his miseries to be more than gender.

Renaldus Columbus, the lecturer in surgery who succeeded Andreas Vesalius at the University of Padua, claimed that he discovered the clitoris at the upper end of the vulva. Thomas Laqueur, in *Making Sex*, wrote that he was a "conquistador in an unknown land." Columbus, the discoverer of the female penis, indubitably for men of science and adventure, said that "since no one has discerned these projections and their workings, if it is permissible to give names to things discovered by me, it should be called the love or sweetness of Venus."

Columbus was cursed with the twisted comic prick of a man and a woman, the ultimate pain of love and pleasure that he would endure in paradise. Women would endure the espied discoveries of an interior penis, as the New World weathered the culture of death from Western civilization.

Christopher Columbus married Dona Felipa Perestrello e Moniz. She was the daughter of Bartholomew Perestrello and Dona Isabel Moniz, two noble and educated families in Portugal. Felipa had one child and died five years after their marriage. Columbus met Felipa in a chapel at Convento dos Santos in Lisbon. One month earlier he saw the blue puppets on the wet stones at the entrance to the same convent.

Columbus lived in Lisbon for eight years; he was encouraged and praised by Beatrice de Luna and other Sephardic Jews. Soon he became a chartmaker and a seaman. He learned from the Portuguese, who were master mariners, how to sail a caravel into the wind, and how to trade with the coastal tribes. He had sailed south to the coast of West Africa, and north to Iceland and Ireland.

Columbus was not an educated man, but he had learned that the earth was round from Francisco de Oliveira, a marine artiste who envisioned the turns of the earth and told stories about silent animals on the islands in the warm western seas. Columbus read the ancient scholars, studied their maps and charts, and harbored an aerial notion to be enriched by the monarchies, and so he laced the bonnet and navigated a politic course west to China and India. He wrote in the margins of the book *Imago Mundi*, by Cardinal Pierre de'Ailly, "The end of Spain and the beginning of India are not far distant but close, and it is evident that this sea is navigable in a few days with a fair wind." Aristotle had reasoned that one could cross the ocean to the Indies.

This stubborn mariner, son of a common weaver, married into noble families; he had endured pain, learned to read and write, encountered the nobles and monarchs, and then he would discover the New World and the stories in his blood.

Dona Isabel Moniz was unaware that she had inherited from her mother the genetic signature of survivance, but she sensed that the bearded chartmaker bore an uncommon vision. She determined this from his manner and countenance, his intensities and solitudes, and his obeisance to the blue puppets at the entrance to the convent.

Columbus encountered the puppets the first time on the island of Corsica; the second time, fifteen years later, at the Convento dos Santos in Lisbon. Dona Felipa was in his memories when he watched the exotic puppeteers. The blue puppets were carved from the same plane trees that were carried by wild storms from the New World. Later he learned that bluish trees had washed ashore on the beaches of islands in the Azores.

Columbus sailed from Lisbon to Galway, Ireland, three years before his marriage. There he heard stories about "a man and beautiful woman" who were adrift on planks from a shipwreck. He wrote in the margin of a book, "Men of Cathay which is toward the Orient have come hither." The woman was tribal, a descendant of the hand talkers, a blue puppet on the storm.

The Portuguese explorer Bartholomew Dias rounded the Cape of Good Hope; he discovered a new route in the spice trade and sucked the wind from the intended sails of the Enterprise of the Indies.

Columbus returned to Spain. He sailed with his son Diego from Lisbon to the port of Palos in Andalusia. Later he presented his warrant of a new and shorter sea route to the Indies, which at that time included Japan and China, to Ferdinand and Isabella, the Sovereigns of Castile. He waited seven years for a decision.

"The most unhappy period in Columbus's life extended over the next six years," wrote Morison in *The Great Explorers*. "He had sustained a continual battle against prejudice, contumely, and sheer indifference. A proud, sensitive man who *knew* that his project would open fresh paths to wealth and for the advancement of Christ's kingdom, he had to endure clownish witticisms and crackpot jests by ignorant courtiers, to be treated like a beggar, even at times to suffer want."

King Ferdinand and Queen Isabella consented on April 17, 1492, to sustain the Enterprise of the Indies and signed the Articles of Capitulations. Don Cristóbal Colón was appointed Admiral of the Ocean Sea over the islands and mainlands that would be "discovered or acquired by his labor and industry," and he "shall take and keep a tenth of all gold, silver, pearls, gems, spices and other merchandise produced or obtained by barter and mining within the limits of these domains, free of all taxes." The document never mentioned the Indies.

Kirkpatrick Sale, in *The Conquest of Paradise*, appreciated the mystery of why "Colón, if he really planned to go to Cathay and the realm of the Grand Kahn, whose magnificence Marco Polo had celebrated, would take with him little trinkets and beads and bells to trade with: that was the sort of truck the Portuguese had used for barter with the tribes who lived along the African coast, not the kind of treasure one would put before an imperial majesty of the likes of the exalted Khan."

The covenant of the enterprise was demeaned by the wealth from the capture of Granada, the last great cultural refuge of the Moors. Ferdinand and Isabella, that same year, built their naval forces and supported the proposed expedition to the Indies.

The Spanish Inquisition, independent of the papal cruelties, punished thousands of people who were sealed as insincere conversos or marranos. Sephardic Jews were driven from the land, some were burned, and their properties were confiscated and used to promote the war on the Moors.

The Moors were once a nomadic culture; the ancient leaders were crossbloods and generous to the hand talkers from the New World. The Moors bear the signature of survivance and remember stories of the blue storm puppets. The centers of their culture, wealth, and splendor were Toledo, Granada, and Seville.

The Admiral of the Ocean Sea was touched with a vision to return to the New World; he would imagine the future and discover, at the same time, the stories in his blood. "Columbus felt predestined, chosen for a mission. He had an uncanny prophetic sense of things that lay in store for him," wrote Gianni Granzotto in *Christopher Columbus*. "In the end he looked past geographers, astronomers and philosophers and sought interlocutors among the prophets."

The *Santa María*, *Pinta*, and *Niña* were outfitted that summer for the voyage; the anchors were raised at dawn on August 3, 1492, and the flagship and two caravels sailed from Palos to the Canary Islands. "Your Highnesses, as Catholic Christians and Princes devoted to the Holy Christian faith and to the spreading of it, and as enemies of the Muslim sect and of all idolatries and heresies, ordered that I should go to the east," Columbus wrote in his journal. "Therefore, after having banished all the Jews from all your Kingdoms and realms . . . Your Highnesses ordered me to go with a sufficient fleet to the said regions of India." The deadline for the expulsion of the Jews from Spain was August 2, 1492, the day before he sailed from Palos.

One month later the boy on watch saluted the dawn, *Bendita sea la luz*, Blessed be the light of day, and the caravels were on an uncharted ocean in a northeast wind. Other historical reasons prevailed, honor, wealth, a shorter route to the land of seductive aromas, but the mariner heard stories in his blood and would return to the New World.

"This day we completely lost sight of land, and many men sighed and wept for fear they would not see it again for a long time," Columbus wrote in his journal on Sunday, September 9, 1492. "I comforted them with great promises of lands and riches."

Two weeks later the crew was worried over the inconstant wind and their distance at sea. "I told them that we are near land and that is what is keeping the sea smooth," he wrote on September 23. "Later, when the sea made up considerably without wind, they were astonished."

"I saw this as a sign from God, and it was very helpful to me. Such a sign has not appeared since Moses led the Jews out of Egypt, and they dared not lay violent hands on him because of the miracle that God had wrought. As with Moses when he led his people out of captivity, my people were humbled by this act of the Almighty."

Columbus was delusional, and he became more and more secluded; his mind was burdened with his vision and pursuit of wealth and stature, and his bones were tired from poses on the sterncastle. The next day he wrote that he was having serious trouble with the crew, "despite the signs of land that we have and those given to us by Almighty God.

"They have said that it is insanity and suicidal on their part to risk their lives following the madness of a foreigner. They have said that not only am I willing to risk my life just to become a great Lord, but that I have deceived them to further my ambition. . . . I am told by a few trusted men that if I persist in going onward, the best course of action will be to throw me into the sea some night."

Birds passed over the flagship and caravels, and then "we saw what appeared to be land to the west, but it was not very distinct." The sailors cheered the seaweeds, and sighted flowers, roseberries, and a carved stick in the water. "We must be very close to landfall, thanks be to God."

Columbus doubled the number of lookouts on October 11. That night, he wrote, "while standing on the sterncastle, I thought I saw a light to the west." The light was "like a little candle rising and falling. . . . I am the first to admit that I was so eager to find land that I did not trust my own senses. . . . I now believe that the light I saw earlier was a sign from God and that it was truly the first positive identification of land."

Columbus saw the blue light of the hand talkers that night in the New World; he saw the radiance of healers from the stories in his blood. "Not since the birth of Christ has there been a light so full of meaning for the human race," wrote Morison in *The Great Explorers*.

Columbus lowered the sails, anchored on the lee, and touched the white coral beach of the New World. "At dawn we saw naked people," he entered in his journal on Friday, October 12, 1492. "I went ashore in the ship's boat. . . . To this island I gave the name *San Salvador* in honor of our Blessed Lord." He unfurled the royal banner with the great green cross and declared possession of the island in the name of the crown.

Guanahaní, the tribal name for the island, ended that ruinous morning with the return of civilization. "No sooner had we concluded the formalities of taking possession of the island than people began to come to the beach, all naked as their mothers bore them, and the women." The tribal people, he wrote in his journal, had "handsome bodies and very fine faces, though their appearance is marred somewhat by very broad heads and foreheads more so than I have ever seen in any other race. . . . Many of the natives paint their faces; others paint their whole bodies; some, only the eyes or nose. Some are painted black, some white, some red; others are of different colors."

Columbus possessed a delusion of grandeur, the tribes with "no iron," the hardwoods, the beaches, the land in sight; he renamed the islands, and continued his mission. He learned from the people that on another island to the south he could "find a king who possesses a lot of gold and has great containers of it." Not only gold, he was told, but precious stones. "God has not failed to provide one perfect day after the other."

Columbus overheard the chatter of wooden puppets, the third time he heard that haunting sound. The moon, in the third quarter, rose at midnight; from the sterncastle he was aroused and pained by the sight of a slender woman in a canoe. Her hands were blue and her breasts were golden, a radiance that was even more seductive in the light of the moon. He touched his crotch to hold the pain of his erection. The storm puppets she carried were carved from the plane tree and their heads were painted blue.

Samana was silent in his cabin; the mouth of the river was calm, but his heart pounded in his ears. She was a hand talker and eased his pain with lust and wild rapture; she released the stories in his blood. He was touched with an unbelievable passion, but never mentioned her in his journal or letters to the monarchs. He wrote that he would "take six of them" when he departed, "in order that they may learn our language." The next day, however, he unwittingly counted her as one of the tribal people on the caravels. On October 14, he wrote in his journal, "Your Highnesses will see this for yourselves when I bring to you the seven that I have taken."

Columbus named Samana in the letter he sealed and released in a storm on his return to the Old World. He revealed in the letter his pleasures with her that night on the flagship anchored at Bahia de Bariay in Oriente Province, Cuba. "The mysteries in my blood vested me on this mission, and the most secret pain that haunted me from childhood ended there on that beach.

"Samana is a silent healer with my spirit, she has taken me into her hands. I am detached with storm puppets in these last words. I fear my soul is with her and will never return to these bones, to give this account before my death at sea. The storm has no fear, the cross waves are blue and we are lost."

On October 13, 1492, the second day in the New World, he wrote, "After sunrise people from San Salvador again began to come to our ships in boats fashioned in one piece from the trunks of trees. . . . I cannot get over the fact of how docile these people are. They have so little to give but will give it all for whatever we give them, if only broken pieces of glass and crockery."

Samana was a hand talker from the stone tavern and the headwaters of the great river. The mariner was touched and transmuted by her blue radiance; his memories turned to bone and stone in the New World. She was a healer, and he was lost in her hands, but she was never tribal because she was not a slave in his name. He wrote in his journal on the first night that the tribal people on the island "ought to be good servants and of good skill, for I see that they repeat very quickly all that is said to them."

"There never crossed the mind of Columbus, or his fellow discoverers and conquistadors, any other notion of relations between Spaniard and American Indian save that of master and slave," wrote Morison in *Admiral of the Ocean Sea*. "So the policy and acts of Columbus for which he alone was responsible began the depopulation of the terrestrial paradise that was Hispaniola in 1492. . . . It never occurred to him that there was anything wrong in this pattern of race relations."

Columbus could have been remembered as the unvarnished slave from the Old World; he avouched his mission to the monarchs, and at the same time he carried the signature of survivance, the unrevealed stories in his blood, and the curse of a clubbed penis. Samana liberated his soul, his stories, and his passion; even so, his search for wealth would never be realized. He died a renounced slave to the monarchs in Vallodolid, Spain, on May 20, 1506, and was first buried in San Francisco de la Santa María de la Antigua.

Stone Columbus dreamed that he sailed on the *Santa María* that Sunday, October 28, 1492, into Bahia de Bariay. Samana danced with the blue puppets on the sterncastle as the flagship entered paradise. The water was deep and clear on the coast, and the broad leaves of the trees reached out to touch the ships near shore at the mouth of the river. The highest leaves wheeled in the lightest wind.

Samana rounded the decks with the puppets; her turns were sudden and silent, her breasts were golden, her thighs a wild radiance. The blue puppets chattered, golden birds bounced in the lower leaves, fish brushed the precious stones, and enormous brown flowers bloomed at dawn, but the dogs were silent and never barked. The tropical trees near shore held the blue shadows of the puppets, the living hollows of their creation.

"I have never seen anything so beautiful," Christopher Columbus wrote that night in his journal. "The country around the river is full of trees, beautiful and green and different from ours, each with flowers and its own kind of fruit. There are many birds of all sizes that sing very sweetly. . . . I took the small boat ashore and approached two houses that I thought belonged to fishermen. The people fled in fear. In one of the houses we found a dog that did not bark.

"It was such a great pleasure to see the verdure and those groves and the birds that it was hard to leave them. This island is the most beautiful I have seen, full of very good harbors and deep rivers, and it appears that there is no tide because the grass on the beach reaches almost to the water."

Columbus lost his soul to a hand talker and puppets that night at Bahia de Bariay, the beauteous harbor and river he named San Salvador. The blue radiance of his birth and the stories in his blood were liberated at last in a burst of passion on the warm beach.

Samana danced once more in silence on the sterncastle. She wore a red cap, trade beads, and bells to tease the Admiral of the Ocean Sea. Her hands were wild, an immortal silence that burst

39

in a blue radiance; the decks were blue, touchwood from the headwaters. The naked men on shore waved to the hand talker; two became puppets, and others were arboreal. Stone was blue in his dream and roamed in a white robe near the mangroves on the coast. The masts of the flagship and caravels were brushed by great golden birds. Samana brushed the decks; the sensuous rounds of her golden thighs bruised the memories of the tormented crew on the *Santa María*.

Columbus was overcome with pleasure, so touched and aroused that he was purblind to the crew and his mission for the first time in his life; nothing mattered that night but the golden thighs of the hand talker. He summoned the torment of his enormous penis, teased the carnal memories of his pained pleasures, but the hand talker healed him with pure lust and a vision of bears, panthers, and brown masters in the brush.

Samana dove from the sterncastle into the shadows at the mouth of the river; a blue radiant stream trailed her to the beach. Columbus removed his scarlet tunic and followed her in the water. That night he abandoned the curve of his pain in her hands and thighs and entered her maw to become a woman, a bear, a hand talker. Her penis was hidden and blue, and his hair burned blue, the best stories in his blood. Samana vanished overnight in the New World.

Christopher Columbus wrote later in his survival letter that he dreamed he had traveled to the source of a great river. He watched his body, erect on the sterncastle the next day; his bones were lost on a mission, his soul was scorned and abandoned with the histories of the Old World. In spirit he had returned to the headwaters of the great river in the New World.

"I weighed anchors this morning to sail westward from this harbor, in order to go to the city where according to the Indians the King dwells," he wrote in his journal on October 29. "After I went three miles, I saw a river with a narrower entrance than the one at San Salvador. To this one I have given the name Rio de la Luna" in honor of his memories of Samana.

Morison wrote in *Admiral of the Ocean Sea* that the "Admiral prepared with pathetic punctilio an embassy to visit the Emperor of China. . . . The official interpreter Louis de Torres, a converted Jew 'who knew Hebrew and Aramaic and even some Arabic,' was made the head of it; and to him were intrusted all the diplomatic paraphernalia: Latin passport, Latin letter of credence from Ferdinand and Isabella, and a royal gift, the nature of which unfortunately we do not know." Louis was told to return in six days.

Columbus was morose and more sullen by the night. His bones and memories ached for the hand talker; she had vanished without a trace but in his memories. Nothing but gold would ease his worries and sense of spiritual separation.

Cruel and bitter ironies abound in the missions of wealth and Old World civilizations. Overnight his discoveries reduced tribal cultures to the status of slaves; at the same time the stories in his blood were liberated by a tribal hand talker.

"This day Martín Alonso Pinzón sailed away with the caravel *Pinta*, without my will or command," Columbus wrote on November 21. He was worried, unable to sleep, and his burdens became more serious with each day of the voyage.

Columbus returned a month later to the coast of Oriente Province near the Windward Passage. Once more he remembered the hand talker and the "sheer pleasure and delight" of her golden thighs. His memories of lust and paradise touched the entries in his journal on November 27; he wrote, "Yesterday at sunset I arrived in the vicinity of Cabo de Campana, but did not anchor even though the sky was clear and the wind light and there were five or six wonderful harbors to the leeward.

"Whenever I enter one of these harbors I am detained by sheer pleasure and delight as I see and marvel at the beauty and freshness of these countries, and I do not want to be delayed in pursuing what I am engaged upon. For all these reasons I stood off the coast last night and beat about until day."

The *Santa María* and the *Niña* remained at anchor in the harbor for six days because of rain and contrary winds. He waited for his luck to return, for a sign, but his troubles had only begun in the New World.

"At the hour of vespers we entered a harbor that I named *Puerto de San Nicolás* in honor of Saint Nicholas because it was his feast day," he wrote on December 6, from Hispaniola. Again, wind and rain delayed his voyage for several days.

Columbus wrote in his journal on December 24, "Among the many Indians who had come to the ship yesterday, telling us about gold on the island and where it could be found, was one who appeared to be better disposed and more friendly. I flattered him, and asked him to go with me to show me the gold mines." The colonial conceit of the gold hunt, even the first celebration in the New World of the birth and radiance of Jesus Christ, was overshadowed by a disaster on Christmas Day.

The *Santa María* was carried by the current and grounded on a coral reef in the Limonade Pass near Hispaniola. The rudder groaned and the seaward swells turned the flagship on the coral and the rocks punched holes in her wooden hull.

Columbus inherited the signature of survivance, discovered a new route to colonial wealth, and was responsible for one of the most notable shipwrecks in history. He concluded that the disaster was predestined, a sign of a wise leader. A tribal leader on the island would show the mariner how to discover gold; his directions would save the Old World mission and culture of death. Morison wrote in *Admiral of the Ocean Sea* that the tribal leader "presented to the Admiral, apparently without ironic intent, a great mask that had golden ears and eyes."

Columbus, determined to overmaster the disaster, wrote a convoluted interpretation in his journal on December 26: "I recognized that Our Lord had caused me to run aground at this place so that I might establish a settlement here. And so many things came to hand here that the disaster was a blessing in disguise. Certainly, if I had not run aground here, I would have kept out to sea without anchoring at this place because it is situated inside a large bay containing two or three bands of shoals."

Ferdinand Columbus, in *The Life of the Admiral*, wrote that his father forgot his grief over the loss of his ship when he was given gold. "God had allowed it to be wrecked in order that he should make a settlement and leave some Christians behind to trade and gather information about the country and its inhabitants, learning their language and entering into relations with the people."

The *Santa María* sank on a mission the tribes would never survive; the Old World lust for gold would silence tribal names and stories in a decade. "Those gold ornaments that seemed so abundant when the Spaniards first came," wrote Morison in *Admiral of the Ocean Sea*, "represented the labor and accumulation of several generations, the Indians' family plate as it were. By this time all had been stripped from the Indians. Gold could now be obtained only by washing it out of the sand and gravel in the beds of rivers and streams, or by a still more laborious process, possible only with directed slave labor. . . . Those who fled to the mountains were hunted with hounds and of those who escaped, starvation and disease took toll, whilst thousands of the poor creatures in desperation took cassava poison to end their miseries."

Christopher Columbus founded *La Villa de la Navidad* on Christmas Day, 1492, the first Old World settlement in the New World. He ordered a fort built on the beach, in honor of the disaster, with the remains of the *Santa María*. The thirty-nine sailors who were the first citizens of the settlement would not survive the year. "Before the shipwreck Columbus had no intention of founding a settlement on his voyage of discovery, for he had only enough men to work his vessels," wrote Morison. "Now, making a settlement answered the question what to do with *Santa María's* people. There was no knowing what had become of *Pinta*, and the forty men from *Santa María* overcrowded little *Niña* with her crew of twenty two."

Columbus had more trouble two weeks later, the first dangerous encounter with tribal people in the New World. The sailors attacked the tribe when they landed on the beach to gather supplies for the return voyage. "The sailors were ready, since I always advised my men to be on guard," he wrote in his journal. "They gave one Indian a great cut on the buttocks and wounded another in the breast with an arrow."

The winter of their return from the New World was cold and the sea was tempestuous; the high and mighty waves crossed the bows of the flagship and caravels from two directions. The decks were beaten by cold water from the Old World and warm winds from the New World. Blue lights burst over the masts and sterncastles.

Columbus heard the blue storm puppets chatter for the last time on the deck. He remembered them near his home, at the convent, on the islands in the New World, and now he watched their graven images rise and beat with each wave, and he reasoned that their dance would balance the ships in the storm.

"Columbus was man enough to admit that he was as frightened as anyone," wrote Morison in *Admiral of the Ocean Sea*. "Jotting down his impressions of these terrible days of tempest, after *Niña* was safely anchored, he admitted that he should never have wavered as he did in trusting divine providence, which already had brought him safe through so many perils, and tribulations, and afforded him the glory of discovering a western route to the Indies. God must have intended that discovery to be of some use to the world."

Columbus worried to his death that his letter would be found at sea, and that he would be tried to defend his sanity over the stories of the storm puppets and a hand talker with golden thighs. "I sealed the parchment in a waxed cloth, tied it very securely, took a large wooden barrel, and placed the parchment in the barrel, without anyone knowing what it was . . . and had it thrown into the sea," he wrote in his journal.

Binn Columbus heard the stories in his letter, and other stories were told at the stone tavern. She heard the stories from his bones and ashes, his partial remains in a silver casket. "He died with lonesome memories," she told the heirs at the headwaters. "Once he dreamed that he was a child in our tribal world."

Samana conceived a daughter that blue night on the beach at Bahia de Bariay in Oriente Province. Samana was born the next summer at the stone tavern near the headwaters of the great river. Samana is a name that has been inherited for more than ten generations of hand talkers on the mount.

CONQUISTADOR CLUB

Felipa Flowers promised Miigis that she would return in time to see the annual laser light show at the stone tavern. She was on another mission to repatriate sacred medicine pouches, this time the bear paw and otter pouches that had been stolen by Henry Rowe Schoolcraft.

Felipa was born in the spring and raised in a narrow house trailer on the White Earth Reservation. As a child she heard the sounds of civilization on an untuned piano and refused to attend a white public school near the reservation. She had inherited the piano and a sense of adventure from her great aunt, a failed novelist, who had lived with a government agent at the turn of the last century. Pianos, lace, and sewing machines were the grand pretensions of civilization at that wicked time of allotments and massive land fraud on reservations.

Felipa overturned the humors of that trailer and overnight became an international fashion model; later she earned a law degree, married, and practiced criminal law out west. Then, one autumn morning nine years into her marriage and practice, she heard that old piano in her memories and decided, then and there, that she would rather poach than represent law and marriage in San Francisco, California. She moved back to witness the last blaze of autumn on the reservation.

Since the *Santa María Casino* sank Felipa has lived in a house trailer once more near the headwaters of the great river with her untuned piano, her daughter Miigis, the mongrel Admire, and Stone Columbus.

Two weeks after the autumn stories at the stone tavern she responded as a tribal lawyer to a notice in a museum magazine and was invited to meet the elusive heir and current owner of the stolen pouches in the Conquistador Club at the Brotherhood of American Explorers in New York.

Felipa posed in a dark brown wool dress with golden braids laced in a floral pattern at the neck and sleeves; she wore bright orange stockings and blue beaded moccasins puckered at the toes, and carried a purple duffel bag on her shoulder. Several men, explorers no doubt, discovered her in the atrium and hailed her to lunch, dinner, and urban adventures.

The chemical chrysanthemums were in perpetual bloom, white and erect in huge black marble containers in the atrium of the building. She picked one bloom with a pink flaw at the instance of his appearance. His introduction, bold and mannered, was rushed and rather elaborate on the elevator; eastern educated, museum associated, and his name was recorded in the esteemed international brotherhood of explorers.

She listened, and was even passive for a time, but then, before she learned that he was an obscure crossblood, she teased him with trickster notions about tribal creation, evil gamblers in the New World, and animal marriages. She told him that the world was united in clever tribal stories, imagination, memories, and that "nothing more could outdare the dreams of the tribal past in me."

Doric Miché resisted spiritualism and tribal trickster stories out of reason as much as he endured the superstitions of his maternal aunts, but he had inherited several medicine pouches and would not buck the manners of the woodland tribes, or a beautiful woman in blue moccasins, when he had something to gain from the bingo monarch and the Heirs of Christopher Columbus.

"The medicine pouches are tribal stories, not capital assets," she said undertone on the elevator to the Conquistador Club, the exclusive penthouse restaurant in the building owned by the

Brotherhood of American Explorers. "What would the old shamans say if they knew their stories were offered for sale by an explorer in New York?"

"The right price are the words that heal," said Doric.

"Even crossbloods can lose their shadows and end up with a twisted mouth," she said and noticed his pale hands on the brass bar in the elevator, and his erect pose. His wrist watch was enchased with diamonds but he wore no rings; his narrow shoes, veal wing tips, turned inward on the verdant monogrammed carpet.

Doric was manicured, an urban explorer, but dandruff marked the collar of his tailored blue blazer. He smiled in silence and watched the numbers rise on the overhead panel.

Felipa read out loud the museum notice that a "distinguished explorer and gentleman heir of the first Indian Agents in the territory of Michigan" would negotiate for sale or trade several "Indian medicine pouches and authentic shamanic paraphernalia from missions and close encounters in the great fur trade."

"Museum prose has few verbs," said Doric.

"How great was the fur trade?" asked Felipa.

"Greater, to be sure, than the power of the shamans," he said as the elevator reached the penthouse restaurant. "The fur trade determined the future of the tribes, fur for sale was worth more than a hide packed with bones, feathers, and superstitions."

"The shamans, the bear and beaver, and now the earth must survive the diseases of the fur trade," she said in monotones. The table was situated in the corner with a panoramic view of the city. "Not so the new fur traders can consume our blood, shadows, and sacred stories."

"Granted, the medicine pouches on the block have increased value because of their association with shamans and the anachronous stories, but the same can be said, with no shame, for rare books and tapestries," he said as he opened a menu. The *Santa María* flagship and two caravels were embossed in abstract representations on the cover. "The salmon comes from our own ponds on tribal land in the northwest."

Doric Michéd pretended to be tribal when his timeworn crossblood heirs served his economic and political interests; otherwise

47

he denied his obscure associations and tribal responsibilities. His eastern identities, wealth and reputation, were based on the trade of tribal remains and ceremonial objects; the remains of the woodland tribes became the measure of his fortune and influence on museum boards. One rumor of his aerial past begot another as lexical loot; alas, he was nominated to brotherhood in that pale and renowned international circle of explorers.

The Brotherhood of American Explorers was established on April 17, 1492, the day that King Ferdinand and Queen Isabella consented to support the voyage of Christopher Columbus. Since then, according to promotional histories, the elitist organization has admitted to membership no more than nine brothers each year. The public notions held that the brothers were explorers to the nines; however, their perfections were not espoused from leather armchairs. The explorers were associated with political power, wealth, righteous patriotism, and covert activities on reservations and in Third World nations with deposits of uranium and other rare minerals.

Doric was the first proclaimed crossblood member in the exclusive circle of explorers; his tribal inheritance was remote, a mere trace removed by at least five generations from a woodland union; the brothers used this trace and his museum contacts on reservations to their political advantage. By nature, the brothers favored the bloodline from John Johnston, a fur trader who was born in Ireland and married a daughter of the Anishinaabe leader Waubojeeg, or White Fisher.

Henry Rowe Schoolcraft, son of a glassmaker from New York and the first Indian Agent in the territory of Michigan, married the crossblood daughter of Johnston and the granddaughter of White Fisher. Jane was educated and fluent in three languages; what her husband learned about the language and stories of the tribe he learned from her relatives. The mission ethnographer, however, seldom cited his sources, and he demonstrated no gratitude to the tribe for his reputation as an expert on the language and culture of the Anishinaabe.

Schoolcraft was celebrated to the nines by the brothers because of his ideas about tribal cultures. The frontier philologist and geologist was pious and moralistic about tribal cultures. The tribes were doomed, he promised, because they would not survive their miseries and moral depravity. He became more concerned with the salvation of the tribes than with their economic development or assimilation. The brotherhood would disagree and revise these priorities.

Schoolcraft lived in mortal fear of the shamans and healers; he wrote that the tribal "mind is bowed under these intellectual fetters, which circumscribe its volitions, and bind it, as effectually as the hooks of iron, which pierce a whirling Hindoo's flesh." He preached that their degeneration was unavoidable because "civilization had more of the principles of endurance and progress than barbarism, because Christianity was superior to paganism; industry to idleness; agriculture to hunting; letters to hieroglyphics; truth to error." He did not see the humor of tribal stories or the Indian as a "man of anticipation."

Doric was enchanted with his race to the nines and assumed, from time to time, the woodland persona of his territorial ancestors; his mother and the unmarried aunts who raised him were direct descendants of Henry Rowe Schoolcraft. The crossblood explorer mastered several casual lectures on the worldviews of the Indian Agents.

"Schoolcraft explored the tribal soul at the end of the fur trade and discovered that there were more words for bears than numbers," he said over the poached salmon.

Doric wiped the masticated sourdough from the rim of the wineglass and continued his lecture. "Their pagan language and the economic environment of the tribe had fostered moral depravities that resisted the wisest missions."

"The bears resisted the missions and lethal pathogens," said Felipa. "Now that, sir, was a wise resistance." She touched him on the wrist and passed him the silver basket of sourdough.

"What you are saying is that resistance is never wise," said Doric.

"Schoolcraft resisted the shamans," said Felipa.

"Schoolcraft learned their language and revealed a moral weakness in their own words," he responded. He folded his hands, mounted them under his broad white chin, and loomed over the table.

Doric explored and discovered but he never retreated to the corner in a conversation; he said as much later and mentioned one banal motto of the brotherhood, "Explore new worlds, discover with impunities, represent with manners, but never retreat from the ownership of land and language."

Felipa was a trickster poacher, the brothers would soon discover, and she would loosen their tongues. She had repatriated hundreds of sacred tribal medicine pouches, masks, creatures, ceremonial feathers, bones, and she has liberated the stories of the shamans from museums and colonial dioramas. The bones and human remains were buried near the stone tavern on the meadow at the House of Life.

She was prosecuted three times in state courts for grand larceny, but in each case the juries found her innocent. She told the juries in her own defense that she was a trickster liberator who poached tribal remains from museums "to atone for the moral corruption of missionaries, anthropologists, archaeonecromancers, their heirs, and the robber barons of sacred tribal sites."

"Schoolcraft stole the medicine pouches," shouted Felipa.

"The shamans pitched their pouches into the lake," said Doric. "My relatives were there to hear conversions and to explore salvations, and to gather a few pouches for the future."

"*Stolen* is the right word," whispered Felipa.

"*Discover* is more accurate," said Doric.

"How much are your discoveries?" asked Felipa.

"Words heal," said Doric.

"The Heirs of Columbus are prepared to negotiate," said Felipa.

"Stone sends me his best negotiator," he said, and then brushed her arm and praised the golden braids on her dress. Doric moved closer and invited her to be discovered, to be more personal in their negotiations over the medicine pouches.

"Show me your pouches then," she shouted over the table. Her voice broke the mannered hush of the Conquistador Club. "Show me how your pouches heal with words."

50

Felipa leaned back from the table and winked at the other men in the restaurant. She shouldered her duffel bag and waited on the edge of the chair. Doric signed the check in silence and then directed her to the exit.

"What do you have in your purple bag?" he asked, and touched seven on the panel. The elevator was hushed, as mannered as the brotherhood at lunch. Doric was suspicious now, on their way to examine the medicine pouches in the museum vault.

"Trickster stones and medicine that would turn the pouches unreal and unseeable," she said and spread the mouth of her duffel open to the explorer. "Watch out my duffel might be a shaking tent."

"Of course, what else?" he said, and leaned over to discover the depths of her duffel; he held his smile until the elevator doors opened. "The vault is to the right."

"Seventh heaven, the prison of the sacred pouches," she said. Felipa walked behind him and counted to measure the distance to the turns, so she could remember the location in stories.

"We have a fail-safe vault with double security codes," he said. "Fingerprint scans and a series of coded numbers." The electronic codes were selective; he could enter the vault and his container, but nothing more. The brotherhood video recorded transactions in the vault.

"The tribes needed a security system," said Felipa.

"But they had more to gain from what they lost," he said, and asked her to wait in a small room near the vault, so that he could enter the secret codes. The room was decorated with pictures of horses and sailboats.

Felipa crossed the steel threshold and entered the museum vault. The tensions of the city and the anxieties of the encounter with robber barons were eased for a moment in the hushed and humidity controlled vault; then she was overcome with memories and stories in her blood.

Doric opened his cabinet and revealed four medicine pouches, two otter, one bear paw, and one that is seldom heard, a sandhill crane pouch. The otter pouches were clean and radiant; the bear paw was creased on the side, a claw was turned under; the crane feathers were bright and honored in stories by tribal orators from the fur trade at Madeline Island in Lake Superior.

Felipa said the otter pouches held the miigis, a sacred cowrie, bones and stones, and creation stories by tribal healers at the time of Jesus Christ and Christopher Columbus. The bear paw pouch held the coarse stories of a shaman tent shaker who drove the missionaries back east with his bad breath and power of transmutation. He would cause tents to shake, even government buildings shuddered, and then the shaman would become a bear and vanish. The more the tent moved and the bear roared, the more the missionaries pleaded for salvation from the touch of shamans in that tribal woodland paradise.

"Here, we can open an otter pouch," said Doric.

"No one but a shaman dares open a sacred pouch," warned Felipa.

"Listen, these pouches have been around for almost two centuries," he said, and smiled. "Naturally, that makes them more valuable, but no power would hang around that long in an animal hide."

"People have been blinded by medicine pouches," said Felipa.

"I opened them last month and examined the contents," he said, and touched the bear paw. "My vision seems to have improved since then, so how can stones and bones blind me?"

"May your mouth be twisted," she said. Felipa heard bears and human voices in the medicine pouches; she was worried that he might open one and reveal the sacred stories in the city.

"Close your eyes," he teased.

"No, not now, but could we open one with a shaman?"

"What do you have in mind?" asked Doric.

"Later, tonight?"

"Who is this shaman, and what does he know about the value of my medicine pouches?" he asked. Doric returned the pouches to the cabinet and then presented a silver casket. "Felipa, this contains the human remains of Christopher Columbus."

"No, how do you know that?"

"Believe me, inside are bones and ashes of the great explorer," he said. The casket was twice the size of a shoe box, polished, bruised, and scarred on the sides. Doric teased the lock with a key but would not open the silver cover. "The casket, as you can see, has been inscribed as the remains of Don Cristóbal Colón."

"Stone Columbus would negotiate," said Felipa.

"The remains were sold to me by a priest who discovered the casket buried at the Cathedral of Santo Domingo," said Doric. "His remains have been moved so many times no one can be sure who is in the casket with him, but in any case our great explorer would start the bids for his remains at one million dollars."

Christopher Columbus was first buried at a monastery in Valladolid, Spain. Then his body was exhumed and moved to a monastery in Seville. Later his remains were moved once more to the Cathedral of Santa Domingo in America. Two centuries later when the French occupied Hispaniola the coffin was moved in haste to Havana. Cuba celebrated independence a century later, and the remains of the explorer were reinterred with a white marble monument at the Cathedral of Seville.

Robert Fuson wrote in *The Log of Christopher Columbus* that when the Cathedral of Santo Domingo was repaired a second coffin was discovered with the inscription "The illustrious and excellent man, Don Cristóbal Colón." Then, as the coffin was removed, "Some of the ashes that fell to the floor during the examination of the remains have found their way to Genoa, Pavia, Rome, New York, and to at least four individuals who may have disposed of their portions in one way or another."

Doric Michéd announced that territorial politics in the New World and the hurried disinterment at the Cathedral of Santa Domingo made it possible for him to discover the partial remains of the Admiral of the Ocean Sea.

"Charles Weer Goff examined the partial remains that were enshrined in a mausoleum in the Cathedral of Santo Domingo," said Doric. He opened a notebook and considered the report. "Goff taught orthopedic surgery at Yale Medical School and reported

53

that the remains 'indicate a robust man with a muscular body build, about sixty eight inches tall, broad shoulders, large head and evidence of considerable gouty osteoarthritis. These findings correlate with known characters of Cristóbal Colón, whose remains they undoubtedly are.' Even more interesting is the lead ball he found in the bone dust. Columbus limped and Goff proved that he had been wounded. He verified a letter dated July 7, 1503, that said, 'The seas were so high that my wound opened itself afresh.'"

Felipa telephoned Stone Columbus at the headwaters that afternoon with the news that Doric Michéd held four radiant medicine pouches and the remains of Don Cristóbal Colón.

"How can that be?" asked Stone.

"Doric is a cannibal, and he could be setting out the pouches as bait for the remains," she said, and printed variations of the name of the adventurer on the hotel room service order form.

"How much does he want for everything?"

"One million on the remains alone," said Felipa.

"The cannibal son baits the sacred."

"He teased over the salmon and pomegranate at lunch, and then he threatened to open the stolen pouches in the vault, but he would not open the silver casket and show me the remains of Columbus," she said. "So, the real problem is how to get into the vault and past the cameras in the building."

Felipa revealed her strategies and told him that she had located an eager tribal tent shaker, a graduate student in comparative literature at Columbus University, who lived near Washington Square in New York.

"Transom has one name and no reservation, but how can he be a tent shaker and a graduate student at the same time?" she asked Stone.

Felipa understood that human contradictions were more believable than salutations and endorsements, but she needed to hear the curious language games of a trickster to be more secure.

"The same way a lawyer is a poacher," said Stone.

"Transom would be an intransitive verb at the headwaters, but out here his real means seem to be hidden in hesitations," said

Felipa. "He said he graduated in Gay Studies from the University of California, Santa Cruz."

"Survivors in the New World," said Stone.

"Redwood metaphors and avuncular discourse," said Felipa. "So, we have one shot at the pouches, and this guy is no more than a hesitation in graduate school."

"Run him past some dogs and see what they say," said Stone.

"The tent shaker and the cannibal, the perfect match for the dogs in the park," she said, and turned over on the bed. The plaster on the ceiling was cracked and cockroaches marched from their seams near the window to their territories in the bathroom.

Felipa was uncertain once more in the cities; she had poached on her own in the past and now she was driven by time and circumstances to depend on a fast-food shaman with one name. She invited two tribal women from the National Tribal Abuse Center to observe the alleged tent shaker and the behavior of the dogs when he entered the park.

Washington Square was crowded at dusk; the wind was brisk, and the people were hurried, even those with dogs. The instincts of urban survival were more intense with the approach of darkness. The tribal women waited for the dogs to respond to the shaman; they had met him once at a reception earlier in the year and would not remember him as a shaman or a trickster. He said he would wear white trousers and have a blue backpack.

Transom crossed the park from the east; the women watched him approach the first dog, a black cocker spaniel with a feathered tail. The dog pointed and then rushed the shaman to nose his crotch. The dog sneezed and turned to a better scent in concrete. Nearer the circle several dogs towed a walker, the perfect test; the shaman leaned to touch and the dogs licked his hands.

Transom had failed, the dogs did not sense the animals a shaman and tent shaker would have in his soul; the dogs snorted his common crotch and licked his normal hands. The dogs might lick him down to the bone and find a trace of bison in disguise.

Felipa tried to avoid him in the park, she would poach on her own that night, but he saw the blue moccasins, shouted, and caught up with her near the chess tables. She was tolerant; she smiled, chatted about the weather, and then as he mentioned his shamanic ecstasies and the hard urban corners in his memories as a bear, the dogs within a block of the park howled and barked. Two dogs leaped over the chess tables and broke their tethers to escape the bear.

Transom touched the bear in his heart, and the urban mongrels were haunted by their wild memories of a beast at dusk; the camp dogs circled the fires with their humans. The sun was on the border, the domestic animal world would be vulnerable that night.

Felipa roared with the bears; she leaped into his arms and bit his ear. The bear in him retreated and left behind a hesitant graduate student with two black stones and cedar in a backpack. Transom and the three tribal women ate dinner together and made their secret plans; they bought a tent, and shamanic paraphernalia for the shake in the vault.

Felipa and Transom arrived late that night with backpacks at the entrance to the Brotherhood of American Explorers. Doric Miché met them in the atrium. He was impatient, concerned about the backpacks, and ordered a search by the security guards. He had expected to discover the pleasures of an exotic tribal woman in blue moccasins, but instead he encountered a pock-marked camper with bad breath and no socks.

"No tents allowed in the vault," announced Doric.

"Since when?" asked Transom.

"This is not a public campground, who are you anyway?"

"Columbia graduate school," answered Transom.

"You said a shaman of some sort would examine the medicine pouches, but we did not agree that a matriculant with a backpack would camp over my property," said Doric.

Felipa towed him behind the chrysanthemums and explained that she was suspicious at first too, "but he does understand medicine pouches, and, unusual to be sure, he is a shaman."

Doric leaned closer to her warm breath as she spoke and agreed at last to allow the shaman to examine the pouches in a tent.

However, there were several conditions: two guards must be present in the vault; the shaman must be alone in the vault with the guards; she would be in the room outside the vault; she must post a five-thousand-dollar bond as good faith.

Felipa wrote a check drawn on the First Tribal Bank of White Earth, the headwaters stone tavern branch. "Watch out," she said, and handed him the check. "You might lose your pouches to a wild tribal woman tonight."

Transom was thin, angular, and weak. He hiked back and forth in the vault unable to assemble the new tent; the instructions, he insisted, were bad translations. He burned cedar to please the manidoo, tribal spirits, and the bears.

The guards came to the rescue of the shaman and had the conical mountain tent together in a few minutes. Doric read the instructions, and then he opened the container and prepared to place the medicine pouches in the tent.

"No, wait, the pouches must be opened together, push the container in the tent," she pleaded. Felipa saw the chance to hear the stories in the pouches and the esoteric silver casket.

"Good idea," he said, and pushed the container into the center of the tent. The shaman undressed, stacked his clothes outside, set two black stones near the pouches, and then the flaps were closed. At last the tent was covered with several thick blankets, and the lights were turned down.

Silence, and then animal noises and human voices came from the tent. The roar of a bear echoed in the vault. Several loud thumps worried the guards. Doric pretended not to be concerned, but he ordered the guards to close and lock the stainless steel barrier gate to the vault.

The tent trembled and then bucked with such wild movements that the blankets were thrown around the vault; one covered a guard at the gate. The bear roared, and other animals and loud voices came from the medicine pouches in the tent. The shouts were in other languages. Several more loud sounds shivered in the concrete, and then silence in the vault.

Doric waited ten minutes, called to the shaman several times, waited a few more minutes, and then ordered the guards to open the tent. Transom the shaman had vanished, and so had the four pouches and the silver casket. The two black stones remained near the container; his clothes and backpack were outside the tent.

Doric shouted at the guards and sounded the emergency alarm system, which he would regret later. The doors were locked, and when the police arrived in a panic they broke the glass doors, locks, and elevators seals to search the building.

Captain Treves Brink was in command of the investigation. He had thick red hair and a massive head with small ears that moved when he laughed. He was brusque at first, ordered more than thirty police officers into the building, and then laughed because he could not resist the chance to search the innermost sanctuaries of the exclusive Brotherhood of American Explorers.

"Now, could we go over this once more?" said Captain Brink. "You said that someone stole some medicine from your vault tonight, is that right, do we have that much right?"

"Medicine pouches," said Doric.

"Do you have a prescription for these medicines?"

"No, you see . . ."

"Now, what about this nude person?" asked Captain Brink.

"He stole my pouches and a silver casket," said Doric.

"Casket, who's in the casket?" asked Captain Brink.

"The partial remains . . ." he said, and stopped.

"What was that?" asked Captain Brink.

"Never mind," said Doric.

"Do we have human remains involved here?"

"None recent," said Doric.

"Has there been a ritual crime here?" asked Captain Brink.

"Yes, he was a shaman," said Doric.

"Who, the man in the silver casket?"

"No, the nude," said Doric.

"Now, once more, you said this woman here in the blue slippers was the mastermind behind the tent in the vault, the nude, and the rest, is that right?" asked Captain Brink.

58

"That's right," said Doric.

"Mister Michéd, our female officers conducted body searches and they found no pouches on her anywhere," said Captain Brink. He laughed and cut the end of a small black cigar.

"Captain, no smoking in the vault please," said a guard.

"Could we step outside?" said Captain Brink.

"She's the one," shouted Doric.

"Felipa Flowers has nothing on her, and you said yourself, and the guards confirmed it, that she was outside the vault with you, and only the guards and the nude were inside the vault, and the video shows that you even helped the nude set the tent," said Captain Brink. He laughed and lighted the cigar.

"Arrest her now," shouted Doric.

"Mister Michéd, we have searched and searched and find no evidence to do that, and besides she has made an official statement and accused you of fraud," said Captain Brink.

"Fraud, what is this?" shouted Doric.

"She claims that you took her check and then reported the medicine pouches stolen to defraud her of her money and property," said Captain Brink.

"That's ridiculous, the check was a bond," said Doric.

"Do you have an agreement to prove this?" asked Captain Brink.

"No, the check was our agreement," said Doric.

"Now, perhaps you should return the check so we can set aside the question of fraud, if the lady would agree to this," said Captain Brink.

"Right," said Doric.

"Do things like this happen around here?" asked Captain Brink.

"This is a theft, not a thing," insisted Doric.

"Of course, but is this the sort of thing the brotherhood of explorers do in the building, or do you climb mountains and sail across oceans in reed boats, and things like that?" asked Captain Brink. He inhaled his cigar and waited for an answer.

Doric was morose, a defeated man in his own exclusive territories; he returned the check in silence. The police ordered photographs of the museum vault, and held as evidence the video record of the nude tent shaker in the vault.

Captain Brink laughed and blew smoke in the atrium. Felipa followed him outside for a private conversation. He was direct, conspiratorial, and pretended to be suspicious of intentions, unlike his dense performance in the vault: "Michéd has no reason to lie to me, and he would not make a fool of himself in front of the police, which invites my suspicion that you and the nude pulled a fast one, but we have no evidence that anything was stolen."

"Nothing was stolen," said Felipa.

"You even stole the crime," he said, and laughed.

"True, but the liberation of our stories is no crime."

"What happened here tonight?" asked Captain Brink.

"The shamans had a bear walk," said Felipa.

"Were there witches in that vault?"

"What kind of witches?" asked Felipa.

"Indian witch doctors," said Captain Brink.

"No, but there were agents," said Felipa.

"What sort of agent?"

"Indian agents and missionaries," said Felipa.

"Right, and who was in the casket?" asked Captain Brink.

"Christopher Columbus," said Felipa.

"Do you need a ride somewhere?"

"I promise to tell you what happened in the vault tonight, the whole story with every detail, if you show me the Statue of Liberty," said Felipa.

Captain Brink laughed, his ears moved with pleasure, and he ordered the driver to arrange for a helicopter to meet them at the lower harbor. He lighted a second cigar and revealed how eager he was to search the building for any reason. "I believed as a child that the great explorers lived in the building with nude women, exotic animals, and pictures of their discoveries."

Felipa told him about the stolen medicine pouches, the silver casket, and the transmutation in the tent; she told him how she tested the shaman in the park, but she would not reveal the location of the pouches. Captain Brink laughed and lighted his third cigar as the helicopter circled the colossal blue statue that clear autumn night in New York.

Transom earned a thousand dollars for his performance as a shaman in the vault and the liberation of tribal stories in the medicine pouches. The pouches were returned to the tribe, and the stories were told once more at the headwaters of the great river.

The Heirs of Christopher Columbus gathered at the stone tavern to open the silver casket. Miigis said she heard the sandhill cranes. Samana would touch the silver, and Binn Columbus would listen to the interior to determine if the partial remains were those of Christopher Columbus. At the bottom of the casket with the bones and ashes the heirs found a lead ball and a silver plate with this inscription: "The last part of the remains of the First Admiral Don Cristóbal Colón, the Discoverer." The remains were buried at the House of Life.

Almost Browne presents his new laser show in the autumn over the stone tavern near the headwaters. Almost is a crossblood who was born in the backseat of a hatchback on a cold and lonesome road to the reservation; he was banished once from the reservation because his laser holotropes, the peace medal transmutations, luminous presidents, and the icewoman terrified tribal families one night.

Almost created Jesus Christ, Joan of Arc, Crazy Horse, and the Statue of Liberty over the stone tavern last year; his laser electroluminations on a clear night are resurrections in the stone. He has created shamans and healers over the reservation, and he has resurrected animals and birds over the cities.

The Heirs of Columbus were situated on their warm stones in the tavern, eager to witness the annual laser creations and resurrections on the night of the new moon. At midnight a blue mast and sails appeared low over the trees in the east; the sails billowed and the laser flagship came closer to the headwaters. The *Santa María* sailed overhead and approached a coral reef in the west. The mongrels barked and the heirs shouted to warn the luminous ships; at the last minute the flagship was saved in the night sky and sailed on to the Indies.

Christopher Columbus rose in his scarlet tunic over the headwaters and walked toward the stone tavern; his hair was white.

Samana the golden hand talker and the blue puppets rose over the red pines, clear, massive, and bright, and danced over the stone tavern with the great adventurer to the *New World* Symphony by Antonín Dvořák. The Admiral of the Ocean Sea leaned down and touched the stones with his immense laser hands. The heirs were in his hands; bears roared in the cedar. Stone danced with the golden hand talker and turned blue in her radiance. That night of the first voyage to the New World was resurrected over the stone tavern.

Christopher Columbus turned to the west and waved to a new ship on the horizon. The *Santa María Casino* with the distinctive cantilevered sterncastle sailed over the stone tavern and lowered a luminous anchor into the headwaters of the great river. The Admiral walked to the flagship and saluted the heirs from the sterncastle.

Browne steadied the laser caravel on the anchor and then surprised the heirs with the recorded broadcast of that favorable court decision on tribal sovereignty; however, he had inserted a reference to a flagship on a laser anchor.

"The notion of sovereignty is not tied to the earth, sovereignty is neither fence nor feathers," the loudspeakers boomed over the headwaters that night. "The very essence of sovereignty is a communal laser. The *Santa María* and the two caravels are luminous sovereign states in the night sky, the first maritime reservation on a laser anchor."

BONE COURTS

The crows debased the dawn with their wicked celebrations in the tender birch. The sun bounced over the panic holes on the spring meadow, and a warm wind rushed the season in the loose willows, the wild cherries; the otter pawed the rim of tenuous ice near the headwaters of the great river, and the heirs were at the wild borders of the New World.

Miigis counted the crows to nine in the birch. Admire, the trusted mongrel with the blue tongue, barked once and then moaned at the crows; she hated their harsh manner and heartless thrust at carrion on the cold black roads to the reservation. She licked and healed an insensible wounded crow last summer, but even so, she has never been at ease with those cruel creatures who announce the demons and bad weather.

Felipa Flowers was awakened by their rave notice that very morning on the meadow. Animosh, the healed crow, beat his beak on the hood of an abandoned automobile; minutes later two stout women in black cutaway coats were on the road. Animosh circled the birch and cawed at the pale women down to the trailer house. Then and there, with taut tongues, the trickster poacher and the heirs were subpoenaed to appear at a hearing in federal court to answer questions about the shamanic repatriation of medicine pouches and human remains.

Doric Miché was shamed because he had compromised the discreet manners of the museum and the privities of his associates, but that was not the real reason he insisted on criminal charges. He had been spurned by the crossblood poacher from the headwaters and was determined to have his day in court; moreover, he was involved in international conspiracies on reservations and would use the court to influence tribal leaders who were concerned about the heirs and rumors of resurrections.

The federal judge, however, denied a criminal indictment and ordered a hearing to consider the issues of ownership and legal standing, jurisdiction, and circumstantial evidence. There was no material evidence to establish a crime, no evidence that the pouches and bones ever existed, and there were no documents to constitute the partial remains of Christopher Columbus. The advertisements and museum notices were conceptual remains, to be sure, but the evidence was indirect, no more than curatorial rumors.

The crows moved from the birch to their silent watch on the black roads as the sun warmed the trailer. The cedar waxwings landed later in the morning, crested, elusive on their return, and minced on the remains of the seasons in the wild fruit trees. Closer to the earth the wind raised the leaves that covered the blue mire over winter and laid bare the wild memories of hidden maidenhair.

The federal hearing opened on the ides of spring to reconsider the remains of the great explorer and the ecstasies of shamans in the same courtroom; the evidence would be stories in the blood and the most original shadow realities ever presented at federal court in Saint Paul, Minnesota.

Stone Columbus and the heirs were celebrated by thousands of radio listeners who heard their stories on late night talk shows. Admiral Luckie White announced the hearing the night before, and she was there that morning with two microphones in hand; she insisted that her voice be separated from those she interviewed.

"Carp Radio live at the federal courts to hear the heirs, the shamans, and the curators put up their dukes over the rights of tribal stories and the remains of the great explorer," said the radio admiral. "Felipa Flowers, in a gorgeous chocolate brown sweater, comes late with Miigis, the luminous child in blue, and Stone, our gene man, who wears his scarlet tunic from those glorious years on the *Santa María Casino*. Admire, the whistling family healer, is at their side, a comic tribal scene that should warm the cold legal hearts inside, as it warms our hearts on radio."

Beatrice Lord marched into the courtroom; she smiled in more than three directions, cleared her throat, and then reviewed the standing of the parties and the issues raised by Doctor Michéd and the Brotherhood of American Explorers. The common rules of evidence were set aside, she announced; the unusual judicial hearing would depend more on imagination than on material representations. She pointed out that this approach would favor tribal consciousness, but warned that the "manners of this hearing would never prevail at a criminal trial."

On the other hand, she would mention later, the laser shows and wild presentation of virtual realities as evidence would have impressed any jury, and might have been admissible at a trial, or at least the denial of such computer technologies, as the new sources of tribal realities, could be used to appeal a conviction.

The sergeant at arms moved the hearing to the largest courtroom when more than a thousand people circled the court building. The judge reserved several rows at the front of the courtroom; the other seats were sold to the first hundred people in line, a new user fee as a spectator in federal court.

Beatrice Lord warned the spectators that a hearing was no less serious than a trial, and then she wheeled back and forth at the polished bench in her highback chair, first to the right and the federal attorneys, and then to the tribal heirs on her left. The black robe shrouded her enormous breasts and thin waist as she moved between the competition. She pushed her short white hair behind her ears, an unconscious habit as she listened to a witness, or she teased the wide bertha collar that she wore in the courtroom. The bertha collars were decorated with embroidered birds, the indicia of her avian memories. Those who stand accused in her courtroom

65

read the birds as emblematic of her sentiments and legal intentions, but lawyers were the last to understand the auspices of birds
and humans.

Felipa wore golden braids and a brown wool sweater at the
hearing; she was even more attractive than usual, a measure of her
success as a fashion model sixteen years earlier, but crows were
the high sign of the hearing. Felipa reminded the heirs that Miigis
had cared for Animosh, the wounded crow, because that morning
the judge wore several splendid crows on her wide collar.

"Doric Michéd initiated this proceeding with a criminal complaint that his pouches and bones had been stolen from a vault at
the Brotherhood of American Explorers," said Judge Lord. "Felipa
Flowers was accused at the scene of the crime, but there was no
evidence and she was not indictable, so the purpose of this hearing
then is to discover what a crime means in this particular case."
Lord held a thin smile over the double entendre of the possessive
pronoun, "his pouches and bones had been stolen."

Hearken, Captain Treves Brink:

Captain Treves Brink was summoned as the first witness. Felipa
and the heirs were surprised that he was there, and worried
because she had told him the stories of the shaman in the vault. "I
was in charge of the entire investigation," he boasted, and then
told the court that "shamanism is not a crime, but a shaman may
have moved heaven and earth in that vault with no evidence, not
even a clear face or fingerprint."

His red hair burned under the fluorescent lights in the courtroom, and his ears moved more than his mouth as he named what
he had discovered as evidence. The captain and the judge were
lovers, but their lust was a secret; he would travel for any reason
to be near his lover in the courtroom. "Better at first sight," he
would plead, and envision her nude over lunch, on the bench, in
the air.

Captain Treves Brink, the last son of marranos in the New
World, was aroused by her decisive tone of voice at a trial, even
more aroused when he was under oath and could respond to her
as a witness. He turned more than one criminal case to their

personal advantage; doubtless he was moved as much by shaman-ism as by the birds on her collar.

"Captain Brink, what about this case?" asked the judge.

"Your honor, the real crime here is that the reported crime was stolen, and we would have indicted with even minimal evidence, but the bones seem to have walked out on their own," said Captain Brink.

"Captain, slow that down for me and the court reporter," said the judge. Lord wheeled closer to the captain on the left; she smiled and leaned over the bench to watch his sensuous ears move.

"Your honor, we have a videotape of the very crime that was stolen, and with your permission we could show the court the evidence we never had," said Captain Brink.

The lights were dimmed in the courtroom, and the monitors presented a static picture of the vault, a mountain tent, two security guards, and a thin naked man with his crotch blurred by video technicians.

"Pray, where are the pouches and bones?" asked Lord.

"Your honor, we never saw them, and as you can see on the monitors, the face of the naked shaman who stole the crime has perished without a trace on all the surveillance video recordings that night," said Captain Brink.

"Crotch and face," said Lord.

"Your honor, our technicians blurred the crotch, as you can see, but his face, we are told by experts, was never there, nothing of his face was ever recorded," said Captain Brink.

"Who is he?" asked Lord.

"Felipa said his name is Transom."

"First or last name?"

"Both, he's some sort of shaman," said the captain as he touched his ear. "Transom, the video phantom, has never been charged with a crime or paid taxes in New York, or else we would have a record in our computers."

"How did he get in the vault?" asked Lord.

"Doctor Michéd, as you can see, helped him pitch the tent."

"Where did he come from?"

"Felipa said he was a graduate student at Columbia University," said Captain Brink. "Naturally, we checked the records for the past decade, and no one with that name has ever been a student there or at other universities in the state."

"No name, no face, no crotch," said Lord.

"No name, and no crime," said Captain Brink.

"No indictable evidence," said Lord.

"Your honor, we even investigated reports of men who said they were shamans and bears and landed more than three thousand names of street people, even a few teachers and executives, but no one ever heard of the shaman Transom," said Captain Brink.

"No face to the crime?"

"No, your honor, but we ordered a computer enhancement of the videotape and discovered more than we ever could have imagined," he said, and his ears were wild with his voice. The judge moved as close as she could to watch his ears.

"Please, we're all eyes, and ears," said Lord.

"Watch the screen, your honor," he said and moved behind the bench to tune the video monitor. "Here, in these enlargements, we discovered what appears to be a shadow, not a face, but a shadow that the technicians cannot explain in scientific terms."

"So, what do we have then, a hoax to hide a shaman and the evidence of a crime, or is this the first video shroud from a vault?" asked Judge Lord.

"No tricks, your honor, the shadow is an unusual video phenomenon that has never been recorded before," he said, and returned to the witness chair. The judge wheeled as close as she could to the captain and folded the embroidered crows on her collar. She was evermore excited by the sound of his serious voice and the movement of his crimson ears.

"Several scientists have reported to us that there is no known cause of the shadow, nothing electric, magnetic, or chemical can explain the shadow on the videotape," said Captain Brink.

"One more burst of radiant energy," said Lord.

"Blue radiance," shouted Truman Columbus.

"Your honor, an unknown radiance is the only explanation that cannot be denied by the scientists, and even more remarkable is that science must turn to the myth of a shroud from time to time to understand something as common as video pictures," said Captain Brink.

"The shroud of what?" asked Lord.

"The trickster of liberty," croaked Truman Columbus.

"Indeed," sighed Lord.

"Maybe the shroud of surveillance," said Captain Brink.

"This video could be a sacred object," said the judge.

"Your honor, there is one more incredible discovery to report," he said, and then turned to the heirs. His ears moved even with the anticipation of his spoken words. "The video shroud, as you can see in this next computer enhancement, reveals the impossible in television transmission, the shadows on that face are three-dimensional."

Federal courtroom number seven was hushed; the judge, the captain, the heirs, and the others at the hearing were astounded to see the trace of a shadow that became a three-dimensional face, a spectrographic enhancement of the video image. That courtroom was brushed once with a blue radiance, and then the face of the shaman perished in static patterns on the monitors.

"Shamans should have legal standing," said Lord.

"Your honor, for obvious reasons we dare not release this enhanced picture as a person wanted for the alleged theft of the bones of Christopher Columbus," said Captain Brink.

"Quite so, but we must hear more to determine the standing of human remains in federal court, and how to treat the repatriation of tribal stories and the sacred animals as a crime."

Beatrice Lord announced a short recess. Captain Brink had his hands under her black robe before she could lock the door to her chambers. They touched and moaned, but the pitch of their lust would come that night at the end of the hearing. The judge returned to the bench, and the sergeant at arms shouted the name of the second witness.

Hearken, Memphis de Panther:

Memphis was invited by the judge to be the second witness at the hearing. The heirs were amused because she had never been in a courtroom, and now she was an attestant to stories in the blood. She laid both black paws on the rail, purred in the witness chair, and waited for the judge to see that she was a panther. She was born to crouch, but she worried that such natural poses would be seen as servile in a courtroom.

"Please, your name for the court record," said Judge Lord.

"Memphis," said the panther.

"Surname, please."

"Memphis, the panther," she posed and purred at the bench.

"Memphis de Panther, would you explain to the court, as best you can, the sense of animal identities that shamans must endure in their visions?" asked Judge Lord.

"We were created by mongrels," said Memphis.

"Yes, mongrel evolution," said Judge Lord.

"No, evolution is a highbred delusion, we were created by a trickster mongrel who disguised the outside of creatures with skin and hair, beaks and ears, but we are animals on hold with interior visions," said Memphis.

"Could you repeat that, please?" asked the judge. Lord strained to listen, but she was distracted by hums and mutters that seemed to come from the side of the bench. She sensed the presence of wild animals, and was surprised when visual memories of her adventures in a game park came to mind. The judge was aroused by the animals and by the captain who was in the aisle at the back of the courtroom. Captain Brink was bothered by the heat and wild sounds; he loosened his necktie and searched the rows for the scent of animals in the courtroom. The judge heard a woman in the witness chair; the heirs saw a panther.

"We are animals disguised as humans," said Memphis.

"Would that be a shaman?" asked the judge.

"The shaman has no disguise," said the panther.

"Really, but shamans are feared," said Lord.

"The animals are feared, not the shamans," said Memphis.

"So, we are animals in disguises then?" asked the judge.

"Yes, and the shaman heals the animals with stories in our blood, not the masks we wear as humans, the mask dies, the stories endure," said the panther. She licked her right paw and then stared at the spectators.

"Would you say that the notions of animals identities, but not human disguises, of course, are what make medicine pouches sacred to the tribe?" asked Judge Lord.

"No, the disguises are sacred," said Memphis. "The animals are stories in our blood, and the stories have power to heal, and the power to heal is comic and has never been sacred."

"Memphis, who is the animal in your blood?" asked Lord.

"The panther," she said, and purred.

"But you don't look like a panther," said the judge. Lord studied her face and tried to imagine the ears and paws of a panther as the witness, but only her golden eyes and nocturnal eyeshine warned the court.

"Memphis is my panther," shouted Miigis.

"The sweet myths of a child," said the judge.

"I dream the crane," said Miigis.

"Yes, and my father was a bear," said Lord.

"You must be a crow," said the panther.

"Really, and why would you say that?"

"Crows are slow to imagine the world," said the panther.

"However, crows are tricksters," said the judge.

"Crows ruin the seasons."

"Rather, crows turn the seasons," said Lord.

"Crows eat dead flesh from the road," said the panther. She hummed to hold her pose as a human. Those in the courtroom who imagined animals in their blood could see the panther, but those who were cowed by their disguises as humans lived in mortal fear of wild animals in a wilderness that was human.

"Your honor, we object to this testimony, the purpose of the hearing is to discover indictable evidence and not to rave over wild animal stories," said the lawyer representing Doric Michéd.

"This is a hearing, not a trial, but your objection is noted," said the judge, and then she directed the panther to continue her wild stories about animals and shamans.

"Crows are human," said the panther.

"You mean crows are my disguise?" said Lord.

"Crows are loose humans on the road."

"Show me your panther," the judge insisted.

"Imagine me as a panther, the rest is natural and wild in the cities," she said, and purred so loud that the bench vibrated. The mongrels outside in the park near the courts building barked at the panther who came loose from a human. Admire and the heirs saw the panther, but the judge and lawyers and most of the spectators demanded too much from science, cold reason, and human disguises to see the eyeshine of animals in stories.

"No real panther would bother with a courtroom," said Lord.

"The trouble with humans is they believe their disguises are real, but not imagination, or their dreams," said the panther. "Once there was a real crossblood who was caught by a vision in the city, and he saw himself in mirrors as a bear, when he looked up from the sink he saw a bear, a dangerous vision that forced him to abandon his human disguise and become the bear in his blood, or else he would be dead in the mirror."

Memphis purred to inspire and animate the memories of the judge; she laid her paws on the bench, showed her canines and incisors, and narrowed the pupils of her golden eyes. Some of the spectators were at last surprised to see a panther as a witness in federal court. The judge was worried and strained; she laughed to consider judicial practices, but she would hold to reason and the best disguises she understood between the nouns and verbs of human existence and the myths of evolution.

Hearken, Binn Columbus:

Binn Columbus testified that she had lived with three unmarried men, two tribal and one pale, and "too many children to count on my hands and toes." Stone is her last born son; his father is a weaver, an idealistic white man with a doctorate in consciousness studies who moved to the reservation, lusted, and wove wool in silence for seven years. "He was a lover, not a word or whimper in that time," she said, and then his silence was ruined when he "shouted at the wicked black flies that summer, and now he shouts into panic holes on the meadow to make up for lost time."

"Please, we are told that you hear trees talk," said Lord.

"Only the hollow ones," said Binn.

"Please explain your powers to the court," said the judge.

"Embroider could become my middle name," she said, and laughed as she eased back the third time in the witness chair. "But our stories come with the stones and the animals, and mine come from folds and containers; on the reservation they call me the shaman of the cracks and hollows.

"I hear the stories that plead to be heard and remembered, the stories that are enclosed and wait in boxes, lonesome bundles, and medicine pouches to be heard once more," she said. Binn unfolded her stout hands and held one to her ear, and then laughed. Her little fingers were turned under from more than seventy hard winters.

Stone responded to her laughter and handed his mother a cloth pouch decorated with beaded flowers. Binn opened the pouch and placed four small leather boxes on the bench near the judge.

"What's with the boxes?" asked Judge Lord.

"Pick a box, any box, for the stories you want to remember, and you can open each one, put a silent thought inside, and you'll see what can be heard," said Binn.

Beatrice Lord was cautious over the boxes, but not by nature. The spectators had their own ideas and brightened the practice with humor. The judge opened one box and imagined crows; over the second box she said the word *panther* three times in her mind. "Two would be enough to argue your point."

Binn wriggled her fingers and leaned over with her ear close to the first box; she opened the leather cover, listened, smiled to the spectators, and then she moved back from the bench. A crow, twice the size of the box, leaped from the opening, flapped and cawed in wild circles in the courtroom. The judge wheeled back from the bench, and the spectators, awed at first, cheered the crow over their heads; some even cawed an avian tune as the bird soared out the double doors at the back of the courtroom.

Binn moved to the second box, and the judge turned to the bench and shouted, "Wait, wait, wait a minute." The spectators laughed at the judge, and then on cue they cheered the judicial caution and personal solicitude over the boxes, as they had the crow in the box. Lord opened the second box, listened, looked inside, and then she leaned back in her chair.

Binn moved the second box to the center of the bench and raised the leather cover. She moved back once more and waited in silence. Admire moaned as a blue light rose from inside the leather box; the light billowed over the bench, brushed a blue trace over the court reporter, and moved closer to the spectators. Then the light became the image of a panther, and the panther hissed, roared, and purred in turns over the spectators. Their wild shouts wasted the panther; the blue radiance turned back to the box. Judge Lord covered her mouth with her hands.

"I hear the stories of animals in their hollows, birds in their nests, and arguments in blood and bone," said Binn. "Christopher Columbus and his heirs hear the stories in their blood, and his bones told me stories about the hand talkers and his twisted dick."

"His what?" asked the judge.

"You know, his twisted cock," said Binn.

"What does that mean?" asked Lord.

"Columbus had a twisted dick, he inherited a curse like the twisted mouth of the evil gossipers," she said. Binn smiled at the judge and then turned to the courtroom; she raised a cocked finger and the spectators cheered once more.

Hearken, Chaine Riel Doumet:

Chaine Riel Doumet was summoned as a private investigator; he had been hired by the tribal government to report on the stone tavern, the wild reparations that could compromise tribal operations and investments, and the genetic notions of the Heirs of Christopher Columbus.

Admiral White interviewed Chaine outside the courtroom and learned that his given name was earned as a football player: "The coach called me chain lightning because of my zigzag runs down the field, and my middle name is inherited from the western métis leader Louis Riel."

Doumet was a retired military intelligence agent who returned to the solitude of the reservation; his survival in those silent years with terrorists and narcotics brokers was tied to his memories of hunting and fishing near the headwaters. The sound of bingo, and then the gene stories, tricked him from retirement; the tribal government, older men with their tongues stuck on cold federal metal, hired him to investigate the casino because they were disconcerted that a crossblood had made a fortune right under their noses, and at the same time the heirs won a court decision on tribal sovereignty.

Later these same tribal leaders would protect the casino members when they learned about the international conspiracies to murder the heirs. Strange as the genetic theories seemed to some people, those who tease their mongrels to breed, for instance, and others who are sustained by trickster stories, or monotheism, or both, the heirs pretend that the singular combinations of bear marriages, curial admonitions, and promises of salvation have reigned the reasons and politics of survivance on the reservation for more than a century. Doumet was hired to report on the heirs two weeks before the end of the *Santa María Casino*.

"Major Doumet, is there a way the court can understand the cultural distinctions between stories and material ownership?" asked Judge Lord.

"Your honor, some tribal people would say that the real world exists and is remembered nowhere else but in stories," he told the judge. Chaine watched the heirs as he talked about tribal experiences. He was there to honor stories in the blood as tribal realities, but not to serve the political interests of the tribe or the military as he had for more than twenty years.

"How is ownership determined?"

"Not with ease in a traditional way, your honor, because the modern idea of ownership is not the same as the tribal sense of possession," said the investigator. "For instance, a stone, a tree, animals, can be possessed, people can be possessed but not owned or sold, and a shaman can liberate the mind from spiritual possession."

"Now, that crow in the box, for instance, that was a trick, of course, but was that more possession and liberation than ownership?" asked Judge Lord.

"Binn Columbus is a generous and compassionate healer, and it seems to me that she has never been possessed or owned, but boxes can be owned and possessed at the same time, but only the stories can be liberated," said Chaine.

"Who owns the crow?"

"No one, not even the crow," said Chaine.

"There we have the problem, the issue of legal standing, you see the crow, the bear, the panther, have no right to representation in court unless these creatures are owned by someone or protected as endangered species," said Judge Lord.

"Stone Columbus has argued the same point about tribal remains, your honor, that medicine pouches and bones are possessed by shamans, but not owned by museums," said Chaine.

"Doctor Michéd claims that he inherited and is the sole owner of the pouches and bones," said the judge. "Shamanic possession seems to be the obscure realities that the court must understand, and with no established rules or precedent."

"Pious intention is one precedent, your honor," said Chaine.

"What do you mean?" asked Lord.

"The ownership of Siva as Nataraja, the King of the Dancers, a statue of the Hindu trinity figure, has been disputed in the Court of Appeal in London," said Chaine. "The High Court ruled at a hearing that the pious intention of a twelfth century notable would remain, and the statue would be returned to the temple where it had been excavated."

"Pious intention would be similar then to a sacred medicine pouch, or human remains," said the judge. "Imagine the argumenta one would hear over the pieties of evidence."

"The court decided that pious intention, or ceremonial consideration and spiritual possession, denied the common states of ownership, however established by discoveries, purchase, or inheritance."

76

"The culture of ownership decides," said Lord.

"No one owns stories," said Chaine.

"Surely the hide of an animal can be owned," said Lord.

"The pouches are stolen, the stories are possessed, and in my mind to receive stolen properties, as museums and collectors do, is an obvious crime, and ignorance of the law is no excuse just because the properties are tribal pouches," said Chaine.

The Heirs of Christopher Columbus cheered his statement, and the spectators were touched by the demonstration. Animosh cawed and soared over the bench and then vanished in the back of the courtroom. Admire barked once at the crow. Memphis purred behind the lawyers in the front rows. Caliban, who would not be a witness, panted and shouted when he could in the back aisles.

"Major Doumet, the issue is one of standing and the problem is hearsay, not pious intention, and there is no evidence, as you know, that the properties in question ever existed, which is why we are here today, to determine if in fact the crime was stolen," said the judge.

"Your honor, the theft of tribal remains is well established, and there is evidence to indict the thieves and those who received stolen properties, but the problem, it seems to me, is over the recognition of stories and natural objects as having standing to argue in court," said Chaine.

"We object," shouted Doric Michéd. He had been advised by his lawyer and associates to remain composed and silent at the hearing, but he became more and more troubled, he said, "by these lies and innuendos about my collection of museum quality pieces."

"Major Doumet, would you explain to the court what is meant by the tribal proposition of a bone court?" asked the judge. Lord heard the idea on the reservation, but she never understood the earmarks of the natural and narrative rights of remains.

"Stone proposed a sovereign bone court on a barge, a new forum to hear and decide disputes over the reburial of human and animal remains, and the court would protect the rights of tribal bones to be represented in court," said Chaine.

"Hence the bone court," said Lord.

77

"Stone and the heirs argue that death is not the end of stories and human rights under the law, or the last rites are never the last words," said Chaine.

"Stone, please come to the bench as a witness," said the judge. Lord praised his wild imagination, and she reminded the spectators that she had announced her landmark bingo sovereignty decision from the sterncastle of the *Santa María Casino*. Lord was proud, and she crowed at dinner parties that she had tamed the bingo savages with sovereignty on an anchor.

Stone was proud, but he was never grateful to politicians and judges for the obvious. "Sovereignty is a natural tribal right, not a benefaction or grant from proud flesh patricians, the heirs are sovereign and the court hears our stories," he told Admiral White. Stone sat in silence in the fourth row with the Heirs of Christopher Columbus.

"Stone would liberate bones," said Lord.

"Stone and the heirs nurture the view that stories are in bones, stones, trees, water, bears, air, everywhere, and stories have natural rights to be heard and liberated," said Chaine.

"However, your tribal metaphors must be tested in legal reasoning and resolved as legal standing in court," said the judge. "Stones and air have a hard time being heard, much less being represented in court."

"Christopher Stone argued in his book *Should Trees Have Standing? Toward Legal Rights for Natural Objects* that streams and forests cannot speak but should have standing in court," said Chaine. "Corporate bodies, universities, churches, and ships at sea cannot speak either, but they have standing and are represented by lawyers."

"The Heirs of Christopher Columbus would argue, then, that bones and medicine pouches should have the right to be heard and represented in court," said the judge. "Stone, the court reporter should understand, is no relation to Stone Columbus."

"Justice William O. Douglas, your honor, reasoned that these arguments would allow 'environmental issues to be litigated before federal agencies or federal courts in the name of the inanimate object' such as trees, streams, tribal pouches and bones," said Chaine.

"Justice Douglas held a tribal view, but the tribes would not isolate the world as inanimate, otherwise he had a natural tone," said the witness. "He would have supported the idea that remains have rights of representation and their own narrative, and he would have overturned the museum policies that sustain the bone robber barons."

"Would he now," said Lord.

"Stone argues that the bone barons steal tribal remains and medicine pouches for science, profits, and entertainment, and the stories of the tribal dead become so much academic chattel," said Chaine.

"Major Doumet, you and the heirs should know that John Rawls pointed out that we possess 'an inviolability founded on justice that even the welfare of society as a whole cannot override,' but the problem here would include the propositions of those whose values prevail in legal standing, those who hear the stories, or those who own the pouches that hold the stories," said Lord.

Hearken, Lappet Tulip Browne:

Lappet Tulip Browne was the second private investigator retained by the tribal government; feminists insisted that the behavior of the heirs be reported by a woman, and with that the tribe hired one of their own and the best investigator.

Lappet was born on the reservation, the granddaughter of the Baron of Patronia; the baronage was a colonial land allotment hoax that became a trickster paradise in one generation. The elders remember her obsession with wind and natural power; the blue wind from the mountains, storms, the pale winter wind on the plains, the power of bears, crows, but seldom has she been moved by the cozenage of men. The stories in her blood are bears and the mightiness of wind.

Tulip was her first nickname on the baronage, a name that described the colors of her skin when she was a child. Her cheeks were translucent at birth, the color of birch at dawn, and she held the natural wild hues of the tulip tree in her hands, even when she was a witness in federal court. Her second nickname, a celebration of her sensual ear lobes, became a given name.

Lappet nurtures miniature wind machines in her new condominium near San Francisco, California. She throws open the windows to the ocean and listens to the wind over the copper blades of nineteen machines, a new paradise of purrs and undertones.

"Major Doumet told me that you would be able to enlighten the court about tribal tricksters since you come from a family of tricksters, and your grandfather was the Baron of Patronia," said Judge Lord.

"The tribe asked me to be a witness at this hearing, and that, your honor, does not include my biography," she said with no humor. Lappet was more severe than her brothers and sisters, some believe, because she was bored, hated men, and had a brilliant mind. She pushed her sleeves back to her elbows and leaned to the side in the witness chair.

"Certainly, would you be that witness now?" asked Lord.

"Tricksters, the court must strain to understand, are not real people, tricksters are figures in stories, no more than the language games of a rich and wild imagination, and in our tribe the trickster is unleashed with a dash of priapean sexism," said Lappet.

"Tricksters have no families?" asked Lord.

"No tribes, no presence," said Lappet.

"Stories, then, are at the core of tribal realities, not original sin, for instance, or service missions," said the judge. Lord was cautious; at times she pretended not to understand the cultural ideas raised by the witnesses.

"Stories and imagination, your honor, but of a certain condition that prescinds discoveries and translations," said Lappet. "Comic situations rather than the tragic conclusions of an individual separated from culture, lost and lonesome in a wilderness."

"Miss Browne, would you please break some of your ideas down with a few definitions for the court reporter," said the judge.

"I am no miss, please," said Lappet.

"Lappet, of course," said Lord.

"The colonists brought wilderness with them and planted their fears in the woodland, and once here their tragic virtues were unloaded with shame, the unnatural consequences of the loss of personal visions on a landscape of primal realities, cruelties of individualism in the church, and the loneliness of civilization," said Lappet.

"Tragic virtues, indeed," said the judge. Lord watched the spectators as the witness pursued the tribal trickster in a tragic world. Some leaned forward on their hands, others were close to sleep; the heirs were tuned to tribal ironies and smiled from time to time. The judge strained to hear the humor in her diction.

"The comic mode is as much an imposed idea as the tragic; the comic is communal nonetheless, and celebrates chance as a condition of experience, over linear prevision, but at the same time myths, rituals, and stories must summon a spiritual balance, an imaginative negotiation in a very dangerous natural world," said Lappet.

"Right, now the heirs and their stories," said Lord.

"The trickster is sound, not substance, the trickster is wind, breath, creation, but not hard or polished in the visual world," said the stern private investigator who heard wind in her visions. She paused in the manner of written words, and then rushed certain verbs, such as being and existence, with her hands raised; otherwise, she resisted the drama of oral expression. "The trickster is seen closer to the real as a presence in dreams, in shamanic ecstasies, masks and tracks."

"We heard about masks as human disguises, but no one mentioned tracks, the tracks of humans and their disguises no doubt," said the judge.

"Tracks are traces, words are traces, and stories hold the wild traces of the told and heard, the sounds of imagination and creation," said Lappet.

"Medicine pouches are traces," said Lord.

"Not the pouches, but the stories," said Lappet.

"Tribal stories and their traces, it seems to me, are not much more than hearsay," said the judge. "Standing would have no significance as a rumor, the legal contentions would be vagarious."

"What does that mean?" asked Lappet.

"Capricious, erratic, unreasonable," said Lord.

"Legal evidence is vagarious," said Lappet.

"Evidence is rational and reason has precedent," said Lord.

"The rules are precedent, and not rumors or stories in the blood," said Lappet. "The rules of a legal culture rule out tribal stories and abolish chance in favor of causative binaries."

"Even languages must have rules," said Lord.

"The languages we understand are games," said Lappet.

"Language can be a prison," said Lord.

"Trickster stories liberate the mind in language games," said Lappet.

"Touché," said the judge. Lappet so impressed the judge that she announced a recess and invited the witness to meet with her in chambers. "You should study the law, your mind is too bright to waste on investigation," said Lord. Lappet told the judge that she was a law school graduate, but that she was not interested in the service of male institutions. "I choose to be a private investigator, to discover stories my way and avoid male domination."

Hearken, Almost Browne:

Almost Browne, the laser trickster of the new tribal world, was the witness the spectators most wanted to see; he was worth the price of admission to the hearing. The lights were dimmed in the courtroom; a laser trickster arose in blue shadows and stood on his enormous toes in the air over the bench. Laser water lapped at his neck, and then blue turds floated close to his nose. First the heirs, and then the spectators, burst into wild laughter over the laser creation in federal court; at last a crow in a robe dove down into the blue laser water and returned to the trickster with a miniature hologram of the *Santa María Casino*.

"Judge Beatrice Lord, the tribal world was created in a language game by a crossblood and a crow on a bingo barge with a sovereign anchor," said Almost Browne.

Almost and Lappet were cousins, descendants of Luster Browne, the panic hole healer and shaman of holophrastic shouts, none other than the Baron of Patronia. Almost was born in a hatchback on a cold road haunted by crows; he heard the realities of his new worlds in stones, stories, birds, bears, and broken machines that his admirers believe account for his leap over the miseries and commonage of the reservation, and into laser technologies with no formal education, his tribal vision comme il faut in the New World.

Almost was raised by mongrels in dead automobiles near the school; he studied astronomy through a sunroof, and learned four "natural deals" from his grandmother; the number of critical deals decreased as she grew older. First, she told him that the wild world was a deal with chance and the best survivors told the best stories; words that became pictures in sound were the second deal; the third best deal was between the real world, the earth, and edible menus in the cities; and the last deal was the liberation of the mind in trickster stories. Almost learned how to read from books that had been burned in a library fire; he sounded the words on the center of the pages, and imagined the others, the words that were burned on the sides. He owned a mobile bookstore on the reservation before he turned to computers and laser holography.

"Would your laser shows be of value to visual anthropology?" asked the judge. Lord seemed to be unaware of the historical tensions between the tribes and social sciences; however, she seldom missed a chance to raise the fever of discourse. "Perhaps you would consider that an oxymoron."

"Anthropology is neither visual nor valuable," said the laser shaman. The heirs frowned and turned in their seats at the mere mention of the value of social science in tribal identities. "We are engaged in a spiritual war with anthropology, they have taken the most prisoners, but the death of their methods is the rise of the tribes and the liberation of our stories."

"John Collier wrote an unusual book called *Visual Anthropology* as a method of research," the judge persisted in the torsion of the social sciences. "He wrote that translation 'serves as a bridge between the visual, and the verbal' and anthropologists have not made use of the visual in the verbal."

Memphis purred and then roared at the back of the courtroom; she would never witness another hearing in court. Admire moaned and barked at crows that flew from the last two leather boxes. The crows cawed to warn the spectators that there were demons and bad weather hidden in the federal court. Animosh arose from a trash basket with carrion in his beak; he landed on the clean bench and beat the meat with his black beak. The judge ordered a recess to remove the burger on the bench and the crows in the courtroom. She reasoned in chambers that new birds on her collar would be a prudent commutation. She wore embroidered cedar waxwings on her return to the bench that afternoon.

"Almost, please show your virtual realities," said Lord.

"Your honor, this is only the second time we have presented our show of shadow realities in public; the first time we started a revolution at a consumer mall," said Almost.

"A revolution in virtual realities?" asked Lord.

"Our realities are shadows, a trace of the real that stimulates sound and the simulation of touch, but our moccasins are better worn than told to show the heart of tribal realities," said the laser shaman. "The realities that were stolen by cold reason and manifest manners."

Almost invited the judge to wear the magic socks and electronic blue moccasins to enter the shadow realities of tribal consciousness. She would resist, of course, but when the police captain promised his protection she consented to be the first judge to travel to the tribal worlds of shadow realities in her own courtroom.

Doric Michéd and his lawyer were convinced that the hearing was the real crime, a farce of federal judicial practices at best. They protested and objected to the legal abuses, but in the end decided that the tribal games and hearsay of the witnesses would have no legal value in a future trial.

"This must be the ultimate moccasin game," said Lord.

"The computer wiindigoo," said the shaman at the bench. He danced as he connected wires, tuned the computers, and tested the moccasins and instruments of a new tribal experience.

The Heirs of Christopher Columbus came down the aisles to the bench for the voyage of the judge. The panther purred, the mongrels moaned and licked their paws, the bears and crows were in their wild memories; the evil lawyer was morose on the other side of the courtroom. Caliban taunted the museum man with his cold odor and strained salutations, but high born evil has never been casual with the tribes.

Binn Columbus fitted the judge with one electronic glove, the magic socks, and blue moccasins. "Your honor, this could be the wave of the future for witnesses," said Binn. The socks and glove were woven with miniature magnetic beads and electrosensitive fibers that were more responsive to touch and muscle movements than flesh and nerves; even blood pressure and perspiration were recorded by the sensors in the magic socks and then translated by the computer into simulated visual realities.

Judge Lord was seated in the witness chair; she admired the puckered blue moccasins. Captain Treves Brink and the heirs were close at her side. Lappet noticed that the crows on her bertha collar had been transformed to cedar waxwings. Stone leaned on the chair behind her and examined the thick white hair on her polished head. The panther purred behind the bench; the sound resonated in the courtroom.

Almost mounted the television goggles over her eyes and balanced the image on the monitors in the courtroom. The heirs and spectators would see what the judge generates with the movement of her head, hands, and feet; the same wild shadow realities on the monitors, but not what the judge sees and experiences in simulated space.

Almost created the woodland near the headwaters as the first visual scene: birch, red pine, bear, the natural meadow, and the great river. The judge entered the shallow water, the source of the river, with one foot, and shiners nibbled at her toes; then she reached down to touch a smooth red stone and pushed under the clear water. She swam close to the bottom of the river, over the bright stones to the last seam at the source.

The spectators watched the monitors in the courtroom, and they could almost hear the touch of the cold river water, the pitch of the birch on the spring wind, the crack of beaver on the pond, and the sound of wicked crows at dawn near the headwaters.

"This is a real vacation," said Lord.

"Tribal simulations, your honor," said Almost.

"The real is the simulation," said Lord.

"Now turn and walk toward the meadow," said the laser shaman. The computers held the biographies of his families at the baronage, and the histories of the panic holes on the meadow near the headwaters. The heirs moved closer to the monitors and shouted at the simulated meadow.

Beatrice Lord leaned back on the meadow and touched the tiniest blue blossoms; her hand was enormous on the monitors. She entered the blue, the heart of a flower, dehiscent pollen, and encountered several brown mites on the stamen. "I could abandon my chambers to be in this tribal place," said the judge. "I have no memories of being so close to the real world."

Almost was concerned because a man at the consumer mall had entered the earth by way of a dandelion and so loved the warm core that he refused to come back to the bright light on the meadow. The laser shaman lured him back with simulations of fast food and cold beer.

"Turn around now and walk toward the red pine in the west," he said, and entered new codes in the computer. The sun was low in the trees, the meadow was warm and crimson.

Lord ran on the meadow down to a wild crescent near a creek with huge boulders. The creek was warm, the source was a rich pond surrounded by enormous ferns. The heated water flowed from the boulders, a warm season in the winter. Then she saw several animals at the pond, deer, otter, beaver, at peace on the shore, but when she saw a bear, she hid behind a tree. The closer the bear came to her, the more the bear became a simulated human, a transformation at the pond. The bear man had red hair, and then the bear became the police captain in shadow realities. Lord leaped on him as he passed the pine, forced him to the ground, and sucked on his sensuous ears. The spectators turned from the simulated captain on the monitors to the captain with the judge in the witness chair. Admire whistled a tune at the simulated headwaters.

Captain Brink was embarrassed and asked the laser shaman to change the images. "Do something now, before she pulls my clothes off," he said in a harsh whisper. Seconds later the judge was in the arms of the bear; the bear seemed so close that the mongrels barked at the monitors, and the crows warned the court.

Almost entered a new shadow code in the computer and the simulated bear at the pond became a bear paw medicine pouch in the museum vault; then he merged that simulation with the video surveillance evidence from the Brotherhood of American Explorers.

Lord was in the shadow realities of the simulated vault with Doric Michéd, two guards, and the trickster shaman named Transom. The guards helped the shaman erect a tent in the vault, and then the judge entered the tent with the nude shaman. The face of the shaman was a mere shadow on the surveillance video, but the judge saw his face inside the tent; however, his face was the same shadow on the monitors in the courtroom. Then the shaman turned to a bear on the monitors; his simulated cheeks and bear ears were covered with more and more black hair. The more the pockmarked shaman shivered, and the tent trembled, the more he became a bear. The judge watched black hair rush over his thin shoulders and down his back.

Lord began to shiver in the chair and on the monitors. The simulated shadow realities on the monitors trembled; the picture was unclear by the time she leaned over to look inside the metal container in the vault. She reached to touch the medicine pouches and the human remains when the container, the pouches, and the shaman burst with a blue radiance and vanished. When the blue faded she was back on the meadow; the natural light of dusk returned to the shadow realities of the headwaters.

"Transom is a bear," she said as she removed the simulation goggles, blue wired moccasins, and magic socks. "The missionaries punished the shamans, biomedicine buried the natural healers, but shadow realities have convinced me that new shamans are on the rise with computers, and the legal issues of standing in federal court could be resolved with simulations."

"The trickster is discovered in shadow realities, the best witness with immortal evidence, but the trickster is never owned or consumed in tribal imagination," said Chaine.

Hearken, Doric Michéd:

Doric Michéd decided at the last minute to be a witness at the hearing. The judge returned to the bench; the heirs laughed with suspicion, and the spectators were pleased that there would be one last performance in the witness chair.

"Mister Michéd, do you have a statement?" asked Lord.

"Yes, your honor, but my presentation is rather unfashionable, there being no crows or laser simulations in my pockets," he said, and smiled at the spectators. He was handsome, casual, manicured, and his manners were restrained but generous; he seemed to be hesitant, uncertain at times, and even concerned over the burdens of the heirs. His pleasant demeanor was more than strategic in the courtroom; as the heirs later observed, his manner was that of an evil gambler, or the wiindigoo, but there were no ice women in the aisles to freeze him at his own best game.

"Please proceed," said Lord.

"I have located the only witness who can and will, no doubt, convince the court that there is indictable evidence to convict Felipa Flowers," said Doric Michéd.

"Mister Michéd, once more, this is an informal hearing, and the court is eager to hear witnesses to resolve the issue of standing and evidence, but this is not a trial," said Lord.

"Your honor, with all due respect, this hearing has been a circus at best, from tribal hearsay, simulated rumors, to that hocus-pocus with magic socks," said Doric.

"Who is your witness?" asked Lord.

"Transom," he said in a loud and clear voice.

"Transom, the shaman, but how can that be?" asked the judge. "Have you withheld evidence to surprise the other witnesses and compromise this court?"

Felipa was relieved that the shaman had been located and was real, to corroborate her stories, and worried at the same time that he was an evil crossblood with a stolen vision, a wiindigoo, a dangerous man who posed as a healer. The spectators craned their necks to see, to hear, and to understand these tensions at the end of the hearing. The heirs waited to counter the wicked moves and manifest manners of the wiindigoo.

Transom came through the doors at the back of the courtroom; he wore a black cape and hood that shrouded his head. The shaman slouched down the aisle and stood beside the witness chair. He was pale, his breath was shallow, and he would not be seated.

"What is your name?" asked Lord.

"Transom Molte, your honor."

"Have you ever been a shaman?" asked Lord.

"Yes, your honor," he said, and lowered the hood with anticipation. He was blond with a thin face. "Rather, I should say that people call on me as an occasional shaman in the cities."

"Were you the person in the vault with your tent the night the bones of Amerigo Vespucci disappeared from the museum of the Brotherhood of American Explorers in New York?" asked Lord.

"Objection, your honor," shouted Doric.

"Correction, the bones of Christopher Columbus," said Lord.

"Yes, that was me."

"What happened to your face?" asked Lord.

"Nothing," he said, and touched his cheeks.

"Your face on the video surveillance tape," said Lord.

"Just can't explain that."

"What happened to the pouches?" asked Lord.

"Felipa Flowers stole them from the vault and then she took them back to the reservation," he said, and turned to avoid the gaze of the heirs and the spectators.

"Please point to that person in the courtroom," said the judge. Lord was certain he was not the shaman when he resisted her instructions to locate the trickster poacher in the courtroom. Moreover, his was not the face she had seen in the shadow realities of the vault.

Felipa Flowers was convinced at first that the witness was indeed the shaman in the vault; he was nervous, but not as hesitant as the real shaman. His cheeks were clear, and he wore socks. The heirs decided to test the witness in the same way the shaman was tested in the park.

Admiral White told the radio audience that the "judge asked the witness about bears, a natural invitation to talk about his way with bears, and when the witness tried to respond, the heirs rounded up seven or eight mongrels outside and ran them down the aisle toward that dubious shaman in the witness chair, to see who would shout or bark chicken. The mongrels punched him with their noses, and he was worried, but the mongrels sensed no bear and wagged around the courtroom. He was nervous beside the chair, because he had no bear stories in his blood. The witness failed the test, he was not a shaman because the mongrels would have gone crazy with fear if he held the vision of a bear."

Doric Michéd was censured by the court for his misrepresentation of evidence and manipulation of a witness; he would have been indicted if the witness had been under oath at a trial, but the hearing was held to discover evidence and information that could be used in a trial. Doric had indeed provided the court with evidence of his demeanor. The heirs saw him as a wiindigoo, and they were not surprised to learn that he was supported by the brotherhood, no matter his evil strategies and discretions.

Binn Columbus, Miigis, and Admire followed the judge to her private chambers when the hearing ended. Binn presented the judge with two leather boxes: "You can hear crows in one box, and sandhill cranes in the other." Miigis gave the judge a pair of blue beaded moccasins, puckered at the toe. "My moccasins dream me to the stone tavern, and you can come too." Admire barked in the chambers; then she licked her blue lips and whistled a tribal tune from the *New World* Symphony, by Antonín Dvořák.

PART TWO

POINT ASSINIKA

MIIGIS CROWNS

Stone Columbus brushed the blue meadow with the last tribal waves of summer birds. He heard the winter in the autumn, the rumors in the pine, the sorrow of birch, red wisps of sumac on the rise, and the eternal crows on the cold, cold roads; he heard the last touch of black flies in the trailer house and honored their slow burn to paradise.

The seasons leave their wild traces in memories at the headwaters; that winter the crows croaked and croaked in the birch. There were wicked stories to be told from the Old World.

Stone meditates on the precarious nature of the seasons to hold back the boreal demons. Tribal tricksters liberate the mind in winter stories, and the ice woman bares a seductive hand of summer at the same time; to be cold and lonesome is to be woundable.

The New World is heard, the tribal world is dreamed and imagined. The Old World is seen, names and stories are stolen, construed, and published. The trickster would be the seasons, neither mortal nor possessed in a cold sentence, neither delivered nor consumed, but heard and created in the crowns of miigis.

Stone hears the rush of buried rivers, the bounce of otter at the seams, and the primal silence of the ice woman, down to his avian bones. He listens to the wind in the cedar, and the seasons come closer and closer to be heard and remembered at the headwaters. The crows abide the demons and warn the heirs at a distance in the birch.

Miigis Flowers, the luminous child named for the sacred cowrie of creation, rescued the first snowflakes on the back of her black mittens. She leaned closer to hear them land on the wool, the creation of a season that would never be the same. She listened with the mongrels to the common touch of winter, and yet the blue snow shoulders on the meadow and the natural crowns near the headwaters became the incautious reach of the tricksters. She turned and rounded the meadow to the cedar; the new snow decorated the clowns she mocked and marched down to the great river.

Miigis was born in the autumn and remembers the seasons from her conception, and from her first winter at the headwaters: the crows that beaded the birch, the sunburst on the low window ice, and the mongrels bounded in the snow shrouds at dusk. She learned to meditate with her father under the cedar. Later that morning the snow crowns loosened on the embowed trees and bashed the tricksters, covered the animals and clowns, and traces of the ice woman.

Felipa was in town with her daughter to deliver wood to the elders and heirs, and to check the mail. She had received a letter from a collector of rare books in England. Miigis turned and brushed the return address, an embossed signature, *Treves Rare Books, Vindos de Portugal, London*, on a foxed envelope.

Pellegrine Treves, the antiquarian book collector, wrote that he had read "with keen interest and much admiration" about the Heirs of Columbus and the recent hearing in federal court. He enclosed a business card and a news article from the *Sunday Times* of London; the inside headline declared that "Red Indians Poach Columbus."

"Dear Madam Flowers," the letter began in a bold cursive hand. "The House of Life, as you most certainly know, is a metaphor that means a burial ground or cemetery in Hebrew. My relatives are buried in a House of Life here, in Spain, Portugal, Italy, Turkey, and in America.

"That you honor your dead with a metaphor from our language would be reason enough to reveal a ceremonial discretion, but the sacred burial site mentioned at the monumental Stone Tavern is the imperative that brings me to write, and to invite your attention to the remains of Pocahontas, otherwise remembered here as Lady Rebecca Rolfe."

Felipa read the letter a second time out loud as she closed the door of the trailer house. "I have acquired, due to unusual circumstances associated with an estate notice, the sealed, authentic remains of Pocahontas, who was thought to have been buried at Gravesend."

"Where is that?" asked Stone.

"Near London," said Felipa.

"Pocahontas at the House of Life," said Stone.

"I would be grateful, for reasons that cannot be wholly explained in this letter, if you would receive the remains of Pocahontas for proper burial by the Heirs of Columbus at the House of Life. Please indicate your interest by return post, and suggest a convenient time that we could arrange to meet soon in London."

"Not in the winter," said Stone.

"Signed, Pellegrine Treves," said Felipa.

"Not with me."

"Listen, he wrote to me," said Felipa.

"Not with me," mocked Miigis.

"Pocahontas has been dead for more than three hundred years," said Stone. "Tell me, how does a book collector end up with her bones anyway?"

"Columbus has been dead . . ."

"What bothers me is that she was never buried in the church that celebrates her conversion and remains, or else this collector is playing a lost tribes number," said Stone.

"He asks for nothing," said Felipa.

"Collectors are never without a need for something," he said. Stone turned to the window in silence. The crows bounced on the highest branches of the birch. His was a spiritual burdened, suspicious of manners and intentions from the Old World, and he wondered why the book collector would not travel to the headwaters with the remains of Pocahontas. "Why does he want you there?"

"Pocahontas is more important than his intentions," she said, and then read the letter a third time, searching for a word, a buried metaphor, that would reveal his avarice, romance, or racial conspiracies.

Felipa repeated the phrase "ceremonial discretion" several more times in various tones and dialects as she answered the invitation. She asked the book collector what he expected in return for the remains. She invited him to a ceremonial burial at the headwaters.

Pellegrine Treves responded that he, indeed, honored the dead and their names, but the "possession of human remains is a serious crime; hence, Lady Rebecca Rolfe is reposed but not abandoned in an uninviting parish. You may be assured that the vicar is unaware of these ironic circumstances. The remains, believed, by most accounts, to be buried in the chancel, are not there. However, she is stored there now by my attention in this instance.

"Your kind invitation would be all but impossible to accept, as much as I would be honored to attend her ceremonial burial at the House of Life." Treves concluded his letter, "Until we meet in London the manner of my acquisition of the remains of Pocahontas shall remain confidential."

Stone insisted that she court the wisest crows and tricksters and not leave the headwaters until the ice broke on the lakes in the spring. The winter was colder than usual, and the ice cracked and thundered late at night for more than two months. At last the river opened past the shallows; the otter pushed the hollow cones loose, and then two lines of geese secured the first shields of water on the lakes.

Miigis was four years old that spring and she could imitate crows, the various songs of more than seventeen birds, the sounds of mongrels, beaver, and the pout of weasels; once she was an otter, and then she turned to the sandhill crane as a vision. She told her mother, "Watch out for the jackdaws on the river, the jackdaws are demons." Miigis dreams the birds and their names in the places her mother travels, an avian vision of tribal landscapes. She was a crane, and jackdaws were a presentiment, not the birds of the headwaters.

Felipa Flowers arrived in London on the same day in March that Pocahontas, weakened with a fever, boarded the *George* anchored at Tower Steps on the River Thames. She stayed at the Belle Sauvage Inn on Ludgate Hill near Fleet Street. She had been in the city several times earlier as a fashion model, a presentation then of aesthetic features to the bourgeoisie, but now she was determined to rescue the remains of a young tribal woman who had died in service to the religious politics of the colonies; she had died in tribute to the noble fashions of the seventeenth century and would be buried at last in the tribal House of Life.

Pellegrine Treves had arranged to meet Felipa at the royal masque performance of *The Vision of Delight*, a spectacular dramatic and musical entertainment to honor the memory of Pocahontas. Treves had ordered a historical costume for her to wear, brocaded red velvet touched with gold and an elaborate white lace shoulder collar, based on an original engraving by Simon de Passe.

Felipa braided her hair with thin golden cords and, as usual, she wore a chocolate brown sweater, wool trousers, and blue moccasins. She would not pretend the time in brocade or red velvet, but she did borrow the splendid fan of three ostrich feathers that was part of the court costume.

Pocahontas was presented at a performance of *The Vision of Delight* and *Christmas, his Mask*, by Ben Jonson, on Twelfth Night at the end of the Christmas season in the Banqueting Hall of Whitehall Palace. King James and Queen Anne danced at the masque in honor of Rebecca Rolfe. Prince Charles, the new Earl of Buckingham, the Earl of Montgomery, Sir Dudley Carleton, ambassador to the Netherlands, John Chamberlain, and others in royal favor attended the masque. Chamberlain wrote to Carleton that "the Virginian woman Pocahontas, with her father's Counsellor hath been with the King, and graciously used. And both she and her assistant well placed at the Masque."

Felipa was overawed by the costumes, the extravagant reproduction of scenes at the revised masque. She danced with kings,
queens, pretenders to the crown, ambassadors, and clowns, and
she was obliged to reveal the new tribal world. Pocahontas, she
imagined, was a curiosity in the company of crown sycophants,
bound in court costumes of the seventeenth century. The garments
alone would have burdened the health of a tribal woman; the bad
air and winter weather silenced a tender breath.

Philip Barbour wrote in *Pocahontas and Her World* that the
spectacular presentations at the masque "would have been incom-
prehensible to almost anyone, the theatrical realism and pyrotech-
nics of such an extravaganza must have seemed the product of
inconceivable sorcery. . . . But this was civilized England. The
lords and ladies of the English court made up the audience."
Pocahontas sat in rigid court dress, "attended by her unimpres-
sionable Indian guard in 'exotic' Indian attire, His Majesty relaxed
in gracious dignity, while Phantasy declaimed:

> Behold a King,
> Whose presence maketh this perpetual *Spring*,
> The glories of which Spring grow in that Bower,
> And are the marks and beauties of his power."

Pellegrine Treves wore a blue mask and a crimson morning coat.
He was stout above his waist with an enormous head and assidu-
ous smile; his tongue teased the wide spaces between his short
teeth, a wild creature in a sensuous cage. His cheeks were loose,
his hands were warm and active, and the low tones of his voice
were secure.

Felipa danced with the book collector twice before she heard
his name, and then she remembered his hands and the assurance
of his voice. "Names at first sight," he explained, "are the last
remembered at a masque."

"Who are these people?" asked Felipa. More than a hundred
men and women were dressed in lace and brocade to mock more
than three centuries of court manners. The music and dancers
were slow, the farthingales were authentic, the alcohol modern,
and the humor was wild in costumes. Teams of men moved in

comic combat, the complete cultural comedians who never touched each other.

"Once or twice a year the book dealers and collectors hold a masque, a spectacular celebration of the past in costumes," said Treves. "We honor you, in this instance, and the memories of Pocahontas."

"Not at first sight," mocked Felipa.

"Our ceremonial discretion," said Treves.

"Could we sit down?"

"Pocahontas was here nearly four centuries ago," he said as he moved through the dancers to a table at the side of the room. "Not at this exact place, of course, because Whitehall Palace was destroyed by fire in 1698." He moved his hands to sound each word, and his tongue pushed behind his teeth. "She boarded a ship on this very day, and tomorrow she would be dead at Gravesend."

Felipa heard that haunting sound of blue puppets. The chatter of their dance wavered over the laughter and music. The cornice and crowns over the entrance turned blue, and then she saw a woman enter with the puppets; she was a hand talker, the blue puppets were wild dancers, and the scarred tables were turned at the masque.

"Pocahontas was a hand talker," said Felipa.

"She was many things to many people, she saved the Virginia Colony from the Starving Time, and she was here to heal the royal wounds of the Old World," said Treves.

"The hand talkers are healers," she said. Felipa told him about the blue puppets and stories in the blood. Panthers purred on the blue tables; the mongrels wore masks, lace, and spiced powders, and danced the gavotte.

"The Old World celebrated death," said Treves.

"Where are the bones?"

"No one else must know," said Treves.

"Where are the bones?"

"Sealed in a church."

"You told me that much in your letter," she said. Felipa considered the advantages of rescuing the remains without the book collector, but the heirs had honored his compassion and romantic association with the House of Life.

"We can drive together," said Treves.

"To where?" asked Felipa.

"Gravesend on the River Thames," said Treves.

"How far from here?" asked Felipa.

"Less than an hour."

"I have a meeting in the morning and would rather travel by train," said Felipa. "Thank you for the offer, but name a time and place where we could meet at Gravesend."

"Tomorrow at the Three Daws on the corner of Crooked Lane and High Street," he said. "Near the Town Pier on the River Thames." Treves repeated the instructions and then asked her about the House of Life and the remains of Christopher Columbus. "Is it true that your people can hear the eternal human past in enclosures?"

Pellegrine Treves, a Sephardic Jew, is a descendant of renowned families who were merchants, traders, hand talkers, and rabbinical scholars in Spain, Portugal, and Turkey. He is related to Moses Mocatta, Abraham de Oliveira, and other seventeenth century founders of the first Sephardic Congregation in London.

Albert Hyamson wrote in *The Sephardim of England* that "the Jews, who left Spain in 1492 and Portugal five years later, settled for the most part in North Africa, Italy, and the Ottoman Empire." The marranos, or forced converts, "settled in increasing numbers in South and Central America and the West Indies where, although still under Spanish and Portuguese rule, they thought that the hand of the Inquisition and of its secular supporters would be lighter," and a number of these refugees escaped persecution in North America. Later, many families moved to New Mexico. Conversos and marranos such as these were the founders of the Sephardi community in England.

King Edward ruled on October 10, 1290, the "expulsion of the Jews from England. Practically every Jew left the country, and it was not until the middle of the seventeenth century that the lawyers gave the opinion that there was no bar to residence of Jews in England."

A few Jews, following the expulsion from Spain in 1492, settled in London. "The presence of this small group soon became known in Spain and protests against the harbouring of its members were made by his Most Catholic Majesty. The marriage of the Prince of Wales and Catherine of Aragon was then being negotiated, and as a part of the agreement Henry VII undertook to break up the small community. . . . In fact it was from the exiles from Portugal of 1496 more than from those from Spain four years earlier that the new Sephardi settlements in England and elsewhere were drawn." They had been prominent in international commerce. Francisco Mendes and his wife, Beatrice de Luna, for instance, were financiers in London and Europe. Christopher Columbus was educated and influenced by marranos when he lived in Lisbon.

The Sephardi communities had endured religious and political persecution, avoidance and expulsion from nations in the Old World. Their heroic travail is shared in memories and literature with tribal cultures of the New World. Sephardi healers and tribal hand talkers bear their stories in the blood; the survivors are buried beside each other in the House of Life.

Samuel Pepys, the seventeenth century bigoted diarist, would have resisted the hand talkers and tribal ceremonies as much as he did a service in a synagogue on Creechurch Lane. He wrote on October 14, 1663, that "in the end they had a prayer for the King, which they pronounced his name in Portuguese; but the prayer, like the rest, in Hebrew. But, Lord! to see the disorder, laughing, sporting, and no attention, but confusion in all their service, more like brutes than people know the true God, would make a man forswear ever seeing them more; and indeed I never did see so much or could have imagined there had been any religion in the whole world so absurdly performed as this. . . ."

Pellegrine Treves, the first, moved to London in the early eighteenth century and married twice. Bathsheba, his second wife, was daughter of Moses de Paiba; their son Pellegrine rose to the rank of Postmaster General after forty years in the service of the East India Company.

The descendants of some of these families were settlers in the New World; some of the heirs might have been removed once more with tribal crossbloods in the harsh politics of race and wealth. Hyamson points out in *The Sephardim of England* that Sir Alexander Cumming, a Scottish lawyer who was "somewhat mentally unstable," moved to South Carolina in 1729; he was "inspired, so it was said, by a dream of his wife. He got himself appointed chief lawgiver of the Cherokee Nation of Indians and in the following year presented seven of the Cherokee chiefs whom he had taken to England to the King and also drew up a sort of British Government, further proposing a Jewish settlement on a large scale on their lands. His proposals included the settlement of three million Jewish families in the Cherokee mountains. . . .

"This project also proved abortive. Apart from Georgia it was not until 1750 that Jews began to settle in South Carolina, but there as independent not assisted immigrants." Lopez de Oliveira and other marranos, newcomers from Old World persecution, established a rabbinate and founded Charles Town. "Seven years later, in 1757, they acquired a cemetery," their first House of Life in the New World.

Pellegrine Treves folded his hands to listen at the masque; however, his hands could not bear the silence and moved into being as she told stories about her past career as a lawyer, her return to the reservation, and the trailer house at the headwaters with Miigis and Stone.

"Even here there is a shaman who knows you," said Treves. "He said you teased the bear in him and scared all the pets at Washington Square in New York."

"What are you saying?" asked Felipa.

"That's all he told me about you," said Treves.

"His name?" demanded Felipa.

"Transom," said Treves.

"Where is he now?" asked Felipa.

"There, on the other side of the room near the door," he said. Treves pointed to a narrow man in a black leather cape; the man wore an enormous beaver felt hat, and his features were disguised by a mustache and thick beard.

"Does he know we are here?" asked Felipa.

"Yes, of course, he was kind enough to make available the news about the hearing, and he gave me your address at the head-waters," said Treves.

"Transom de Bear," she shouted twice from the table. He turned and moved toward her through the dancers. "He's a shaman who could vanish in his own clothes." She waved with excitement, but somehow, in the motion of dancers, and the shudder of the lights in the room, he vanished at the masque.

"He must be at the entrance," said Treves.

"Transom is no more," she said. Felipa would not reveal her worries, but she asked the book collector to escort her back to the Belle Sauvage Inn.

London was abandoned at that late hour; the lonesome horses, statues and stones carved in a lost summer, crewed at the circles under the waxen lights. Colors were hidden at the cold borders; here and there banners in blood and gold decorated a pallid facade to honor the glories of the crown.

Felipa telephoned the headwaters that night from under the covers of the narrow bed in her cold room. "Pellegrine Treves leans too much on manners, but he is an honest man," she told Stone.

"What does he say?" asked Stone.

"He wore a blue mask and talked with his hands," said Felipa.

"That's a start," said Stone.

"He listens," she said. "He even convinced me that Transom was at the party, dressed in a cape, and he said the shaman gave him our address."

"Who was he, then?"

"Transom could never grow a beard worth mentioning, he was too close to the bone, but the disguise worked on the book collector," said Felipa.

"The people in his books," said Stone.

"The imposter vanished when I called to him, and that worries me," said Felipa. "Transom was much too insecure to avoid me, he needed the attention of women and the acceptance of the tribe."

"So, what happens now?"

"Treves wants me to meet him late tomorrow at Gravesend," she said. "I'm sure there's more to the name than the place, but someone said it means the end of the grove."

"Better at first sight," said Stone.

"Where did you hear that?"

"Captain Treves Brink, who else?"

"Pellegrine Treves, names at first sight," said Felipa.

"So, where is Pocahontas?"

"Somewhere at Gravesend," she said, "but he won't tell me until we meet tomorrow at the Three Daws, and even then he might direct me to the church, or wherever, rather than handing over the bones himself, because he seems to be worried about criminal possession."

"Carry a sprig of white pine," said Stone.

"Naturally," she said. Felipa and the heirs carry a cut of white pine when they travel alone, as bald eagles have fresh sprigs in their nests. "If only white pine could heat this room."

"Where is Gravesend?" asked Stone.

"Near London on the River Thames," said Felipa.

"Call me the minute you hold her remains," said Stone.

"Listen to the mistle thrush," said Miigis.

"Did you see them?" asked Felipa.

"I dream you with mistle thrush last night," said Miigis.

"Miigis, count the crows in the morning until you see me in a few more days, and dream me with the birds and Admire," said Felipa.

The sun was smothered on the rise over London Bridge. The moist breeze carried the scent of sour limestone, carbon monoxide, pigeons, soiled cardboard, and burned plastics, down to the cold reach of the River Thames.

Felipa visited with a barrister at the Royal Courts of Justice to discuss the "pious intentions" decision over the ownership of the King of the Dancers statue, and then she ate lunch in a cafe at Neals Yard near Covent Gardens. That afternoon she inquired of Pellegrine Treves at an antiquarian bookstore on Cecil Street; she was reassured that he was the "most reputable and distinguished antiquarian book collector in the world."

Later she walked down Middle Temple Lane, around the gardens, east on Victoria Embankment to New Bridge Street near the

Belle Sauvage Inn, and used the Underground between Blackfriars and Monument. She walked across London Bridge, over the River Thames, and on the north bank saw the haunting Tower of London; closer, she saluted the twin gothic bascules of Tower Bridge. The Tower of London, built in the eleventh century, was a royal residence when Pocahontas visited London. She boarded the *George* near the Tower of London that same day in 1617.

Felipa walked to London Bridge Station and boarded a British Rail train to Gravesend. The sun was low over the River Thames. She walked from the station to Stone Street, across King Street, and continued toward the Town Pier on Princes Street. She turned at St. George's Parish Church and admired in the garden the bronze statue of Princess Pocahontas, a replica of a statue in Jamestown, Virginia.

Gravesend was once the pilot port to London. The long ferry carried passengers between the two cities for more than four centuries. Black Elk, as others on ships from the New World, landed at Gravesend. Buffalo Bill Cody had hired more than a hundred tribal people for his Wild West Show, and chartered the steamer *State of Nebraska* for an exhibition in London.

Gravesend smelled of the sea, the pale mire on shore, and the scent of chalk and lime burners once located in Slave's Alley. The waterline was haunted by white chalkers, and river pilots, and the explorers who set sail for other worlds from the town piers. Sir Martin Frobisher attempted three times to discover the Northwest Passage. John Cabot also sailed from Gravesend; he discovered Cape Breton, which he thought was Asia, in 1497.

Richard Church wrote in *Kent* that "Gravesend is a maritime, one might say a saline, place. There is a robust, hornpipe character about its people. One expects to see a parrot in every front room, and a tattooist's shop round every corner." Pocahontas saw the last bright lights at Gravesend.

Pocahontas was born in 1595. Powhatan, the overlord of a tribal crescent on Chesapeake Bay, and his wife, Winganuske, named their daughter Matoaka, a tender metaphor. Pocahontas was a dubious colonial nickname that had sexual overtones, "a playful little girl." She married Kocoum in the tribal manner. Then, a short time later, she was betrothed to John Rolfe, a tobacco grower, and married on April 5, 1614, by Reverend Richard Buck. Grace Steele Woodward wrote in *Pocahontas* that the guests were "summoned to the ceremony by church bells, whose chimes echoed pleasantly on the Jamestown air."

The first converted tribal bride in the New World wore a "tunic of white Dacca muslin" and a "flowing veil and long robe of rich material. Her father sent her a chain of pearls and Sir Thomas Dale gave her an Italian ring," wrote Carolyn Thomas Foreman in *Indians Abroad*. The couple lived in a house on the shore of the James River near Bermuda Hundred. Rolfe was appointed Secretary of the Virginia Colony. Thomas Rolfe, their only child, was born a year later.

Some of these men of the Old World would have been dismissed, as their wives and children were tribal, but in the New World colonial survival condoned, in one instance, racial intermarriage. The Book of Ezra provides severe measures against mixed marriages. Ezra the priest said, "You have broken faith in marrying foreign women."

Alexander Whitaker, an educated and pious man, wrote to a minister of the Blackfriars in London: Pocahontas married "an honest and discreet English gentleman, Master Rolfe, and that after she openly renounced her country idolatry, confessed the faith of Jesus Christ, and was baptized; which thing Sir Thomas Dale had labored a long time to ground in her."

Pocahontas, John Rolfe, their son, and others sailed on the *Treasurer* and arrived at Plymouth on June 12, 1616. They stayed at the Belle Sauvage Inn on Ludgate Hill in London. She was praised by distinguished gentlemen, entertained, honored by royalty, and nine months later prepared to return to the civilization of the New World.

Pocahontas had been weakened by social observance and disease; she boarded the *George* with her husband and son. The ship sailed on the River Thames twenty five miles to Gravesend. There, "in painful simplicity," wrote Philip Barbour in *Pocahontas and Her World*, "as spring came to England, Princess Pocahontas begged to be taken ashore. She was deathly ill. . . . The *George* dropped anchor, and Pocahontas was carried onto the little wharf. A hundred yards or so away, the three-story inn rose massively before them. Pocahontas was hurried to a room, and a doctor was summoned—that much, at least, may be surmised, for there is no record.

"It was too late. Climate, that had killed many an Englishman in Virginia, took the life of Pocahontas in England. Climate, and a broken heart. There is no need to postulate some epidemic, some disease."

Charles Ap Thomas, in *Ye True Narrative of ye Princess Pocahontas*, wrote that she was buried "on the site, or in the close vicinity, of the then disused old parish church of Saint Marie's." Later her burial was ensured in the chancel of St. George's Parish Church; the register reveals that "Rebecca Wrothe wyff of Thomas Wroth gent a Virginia lady borne, here is buried in ye chanuncell." There has been no evidence to support the rumors that her remains were stolen by body snatchers in the seventeenth century and sold to collectors in London.

Miigis saw birds in the wild time of her dreams, and there in the garden near the church, a mistle thrush turned on the highest branch of a tree. The low sun brightened the brown thrush and the clock on the church tower. Felipa heard the thrush and watched her shadow lean with Pocahontas over the lush garden, broken on the iron gate; the sun wavered as the shadows reached out over the cold black road.

The mistle thrush is a storm cock, the watchers and dreamers say, as in the winter the songs, the sound of flute notes, are heard to warn of storms. The wind raised the mistle thrush on the branch, and the song wavered with the shadows. Then the shadows vanished in the garden.

Felipa walked down West Street past the New Falcon Inn to Crooked Lane; there, on the corner, across from the Pier Hotel, was the Three Daws on the River Thames.

Pellegrine Treves was seated at a small table near the window. "I just arrived myself," he said, and with chivalrous manners held her coat and directed her to a chair at the table. He ordered sherry, and she ordered a pint of bitter. In the distance, from the liquor bar at the entrance, she heard the matriclinous rancor and the haunting pities of Sinéad O'Connor.

"The weather has turned," said Treves.

"Yes, the mistle thrush sang down the sun," said Felipa.

"Are you a dedicated bird watcher?"

"My daughter dreams birds," said Felipa.

"The mistle cock, as you know, is our weather bird," said Treves.

"Yes, the storm cock," said Felipa.

"You were at the church then?"

"That statue laid a lonesome shadow," said Felipa.

"Lonesome, indeed," said Treves.

"The invention of a tourist civilization," said Felipa.

"Quite, not a pose in the proper sense, but a rather cruel and arrested romance, as if she might burst from the hollow bronze in full stride back to the New World," said Treves.

"She would be walking north," said Felipa.

"Indeed, and her remains are hidden at the church," said Treves.

"Hidden in the chancel after all?"

"No, her remains were first stolen from the rector's vault when a new chancel was built a century ago, and over the years, stolen once or twice again from the secret owners, but then, as others learned of my interests in rare books about American Indians, it was inevitable that the remains of Pocahontas would be offered to me," said Treves.

"But why hide her at the church?"

"Pocahontas touched me as a child, she was beautiful, courageous, so persecuted by manners, and she died so young, lonesome for her homeland," said Treves.

"The noble savage," she said in a cold and critical tone. Felipa resisted his romantic revisions of tribal cultures and women, but the tone of her mordant response was unclear. "Too much romance subdues our humor and miseries."

"I was in love at first sight of her in portraits, and then my adolescent love matured in the most unusual and personal way, as I learned that my relatives must have danced with her at the masque, she was touched by my family," he said, and pressed his hands on the table. "I was determined to prove that our families were related, that my relatives married hers in the New World, that we were of the same tribe, that we would be united in the House of Life."

"Who stole her bones?" asked Felipa.

"I considered the return of her remains to the church where she might have been buried, but then the matter was settled when I read about the headwaters and the Heirs of Columbus," said Treves.

"So, you could have delivered her remains to me at the masque or at the Belle Sauvage Inn," she said. "Instead, here we are near the inn of her death."

"Indeed, but the truth of the matter is my fear of death and human remains," he said, and moaned. Treves pressed his hands on the table each time he mentioned the remains of the woman he loved. "I could not bear to overturn my love of her with the reality of her remains under my arm." Treves cleared his throat. "You see, it was quite enough that she was locked in the boot of my car, but once at the church it took me hours and hours of consideration to overcome my fear and resistance to hide her remains in the church."

"Vindos de Portugal, what does that mean?" asked Felipa.

"The refugees, we were identified as marranos and refugees," he said. Treves was relieved that she had turned the conversation. "Now, of course, the adversities of the past are measures of honor and compassion."

"Marvelous, the turns of language," said Felipa.

"Indeed, however bold the revisions, there is much to admire in a civilization that turns the real world of rubbish tips into civic amenities, and other royal euphemisms for common trash."

"What books do you collect?" asked Felipa.

"I started my collection more than forty years ago with doublure and fore-edged painted books, but the obscure pastoral scenes did not hold my interest for long," said Treves.

"How is that done?" she asked. Felipa pretended that she had at least a basic knowledge of antiquarian books. "I mean, how many methods were there?"

"The edges of the pages are fanned and then painted, so that when the book is closed, unfanned as it were, the scenes on the edges are not seen," said Treves.

"But your interest turned to American Indians," said Felipa.

"Yes, but not straight away," he said. "I built a very good collection of first edition association copies, mostly in fiction, but with a few others in history and philosophy."

"Indian novels?"

"Yes, several first editions with signatures by James Welch, Louise Erdrich, Leslie Silko, and a special copy dedicated to me by the novelist and book collector Thomas King, but the most unusual association edition in my collection is *The Voice in the Margin*, by Arnold Krupat," said Treves.

"Krupat said he was an Indian?"

"No, not really, you see a first edition of his book was sold at public auction with marginal notes by N. Scott Momaday, winner of the Pulitzer prize, as you know," said Treves.

"He wrote *The House Made of Dawn*, *The Way to Rainy Mountain*, and, as you know, he won the first Native American Literature prize," said Felipa.

"Yes, I have signed copies of those and a first edition of his second novel the *Ancient Child*, as well as his autobiography, *The Names*, with notes he made for a public reading," said Treves.

"What does he say about Krupat?" asked Felipa.

"Well, as the marginal notes are attributed to Momaday, one would say he was not pleased with Krupat, rather captious, but ironies abound even in the staid relations of antiquarian book auctions," he said. "The marginal notes, you see, were by another distinguished novelist who pretended to be Momaday." Treves touched the pleasures of antiquarian tenure, the arcanum of association literature, the subdued glories of a book collector.

"What Momaday might have written?"

"Indeed, and the book was returned to auction," he said. "I acquired it at a real bargain and learned later that the marginal notes were by another notable novelist, so the copy has a double association, you might say."

"Who wrote the notes?" asked Felipa.

"That much is confidential," said Treves.

"The margins, then," said Felipa.

"Krupat wrote that Momaday offered an 'invariant poetic voice that everywhere commits itself to subsuming and translating all other voices,' and so on, to which the novelist made a marginal note, 'but not enough to subsume your arrogance and dialogic domination.'"

"Sounds like an esoteric word war to me, but at the same time the sense of oral stories in the printed word is mythic, the remembered poet over the noted critic," said Felipa.

"Indeed, but Krupat's discussion of 'racial memory' drew the sharpest marginal responses," said Treves. "The novelist noted, 'Krupat gives head to footnotes, how would he know about tribal memories?'"

"Krupat would be the trickster on the margins," said Felipa.

"The book is great, and the notes are cruel," said Treves.

"The politics of tribal creation stories never ends," said Felipa.

"Most of the editions in my collection are valued for their association rather than racial politics," he said. Treves checked his wrist watch several times. "Forgive me, but we must be at the church on the hour."

"Whatever you say," said Felipa.

"The church ladies open the door at seven o'clock for about fifteen minutes for the cleaners, otherwise the church is locked but for services," said Treves.

"So, tell me about your other books then," said Felipa.

"You're too kind," said Treves.

"No, really, the most interesting editions."

"I have acquired several novels and manuscripts by William Faulkner, first editions of *As I Lay Dying, Go Down, Moses*, and others, with perfect dust jackets, and a signed first edition of *Look Homeward, Angel*, by Thomas Wolfe," said Treves.

"How about Indian Bibles?" asked Felipa.

"John Eliot's famous *Upbiblum God* is in my collection," said Treves.

"How much is that worth?"

"You must mean at auction?"

"Yes," said Felipa.

"The 1663 Cambridge edition might bring more than thirty thousand dollars," said Treves. He smiled, folded his hands on the table, and checked the time. "We have forty minutes."

"Do you buy at auctions?" asked Felipa.

"Seldom, my collection is more selective and personal, for instance, several years ago I acquired from an antiquarian dealer the twenty volume set of *The North American Indian*, by Edward Curtis, with association signatures of the author and President Theodore Roosevelt," said Treves.

"Fascinating, but what's your most valuable edition?"

"The *Manabosho Bestiary Curiosa*, no doubt," said Treves.

"Stone told me about that book," said Felipa.

"A rare anonymous manuscript collection of wild erotic stories with original drawings in color of the vainglorious trickster posing with his enormous penis," he said. "The edition is cased and published at Madeline Island, Lake Superior, in 1653."

"Schoolcraft must be the author," said Felipa.

"No, he came later," said Treves.

"Could this be the work of a missionary?"

"Now there is a trickster story," said Treves.

"Stone would like a copy," said Felipa.

"Several publishers have invited me, over the years, to consider a special facsimile first edition of the manuscript, cased and stained," said Treves.

"How many manuscripts are there?" asked Felipa.

"One, no more," said Treves.

"Incredible, but how can it be that you own the only copy of a tribal manuscript that was written more than three centuries ago?" asked Felipa.

"An estate sale in London," said Treves.

"How does the only copy end up here?" asked Felipa.

"George Catlin may have obtained the manuscript from the Ojibway Indians who were brought to Paris by a Canadian, or at least that is one of the theories of how *Manabosho Bestiary Curiosa* landed in England, but even more complicated is the date of publication in 1653," said Treves.

112

"The trickster calendar," said Felipa.

"I have been told that the trickster bestiary was published as a tribal antidote to *Catechism in the Indian Language*, by John Eliot, the first book printed in an Indian language that same year," said Treves.

"Now that makes sense in trickster time," said Felipa.

"Prurient interests alone would seem insufficient motivation for a cleric or colonial factor to return with such an erotic manuscript on his own," said Treves.

"Black Elk might have brought the manuscript," said Felipa. "He was here with Buffalo Bill Cody in the Wild West Show and met Queen Victoria."

"I understand the Sioux and Ojibways were enemies," said Treves. "So why would he have possession of the bestiary, unless, of course, he intended to use the manuscript as a trickster coup count in the Old World?"

"Trickster stories and tribal enemies are not the same," said Felipa.

"Indeed, but someone would have remembered the manuscript," said Treves. He checked the time once more and paid the waiter for the beer and sherry.

"Have the ladies arrived?" asked Felipa.

"They should do in a few minutes," he said, and held her coat. Treves was a familiar face in the Three Daws. Once or twice a month he visits with rare book collectors, and a retired captain of a ship. Even as a child he was eager to hear stories about the sea, but he has never collected books about exploration or ships.

The River Thames soughed on the cold moist air, and the lights of the passenger ferry wavered in the distance. Treves turned and explained as they walked that the remains of Pocahontas were sealed in a narrow black metal case and hidden in a storage closet under the stairs at St. George's Parish Church.

"The closet is to the left as you enter the church," he said. "You enter through a small door near the toilets, so be careful not to hit your head."

"As *you* enter?"

"Yes, you must understand how much this has troubled me, and my only comfort now is that you will bury her in the House of Life," said Treves.

"Where will you be?" asked Felipa.

"Outside, in the garden by the statue," said Treves.

"You won't leave me alone?"

"Not until you have her remains in hand," said Treves.

"What about the ladies?" asked Felipa.

"The ladies will probably be in the small kitchen area to the left, if not, then appreciate the stained glass windows for a few minutes," said Treves.

Felipa listened at the black double doors; inside, the ladies raised their voices over a recent wedding. Treves waited near the statue in the garden. The trickster poacher pushed the door and entered the cold church. The ladies smiled on cue and directed the tourist to the stained glass at the sides of the chancel. Felipa studied the arched windows, but she was poised to rescue the remains of Pocahontas.

The two memorial windows were presented by the Colonial Dames of America in 1914. The Ruth window on the left shows Pocahontas in a rigid court costume, with a wide lace collar and an ostrich feather fan in her right hand; the stained glass image is similar to the seventeenth century engraved portrait by Simon de Passe, the only likeness made during her life, and the portrait of Lady Rebecca in the National Portrait Gallery. A facsimile of the engraving was published as the frontispiece to the *Generall Historie*, by John Smith, in London, 1624.

The Rebecca window on the right of the chancel shows Pocahontas in the lower right corner in baptismal attire, the representation of the first tribal convert married and buried as a curiosity in the traditions of the Old World.

Felipa heard the ladies in the kitchen area; she moved close to the wall and found the storage closet door open, and one of the ladies was inside. "The loo is over there, dear," she said, and pointed.

"Yes, thank you," she said, and smiled. Felipa waited in the toilet until she heard the storage door close; then she flushed the toilet and dashed to the area under the stairs. She found the black unmarked metal case behind a stack of portraits. The seams of the heavy case were sealed with wax, the only indication that it contained human remains.

Felipa walked out of the church unseen, closed the black door, and rushed to the statue of Pocahontas. "The ladies were too kind," she said out of breath as she rounded the statue, but no one was there. Pellegrine Treves had vanished in the night.

Felipa saw several people approaching the church on the garden path; she turned behind the statue and ran on the wet grass to the western gate at the back of the church. She had rescued a tribal woman from the cruelties of more than three centuries of civilization; she was at peace, unconcerned, and lonesome for the heirs at the headwaters. She closed the iron gate and walked back toward the train station on Princes Street.

She remembered the description of the port town, a saline place with a hornpipe character; she whistled a tune from the *New World* Symphony, by Antonín Dvořák, and tasted the saline air of Gravesend.

Felipa walked close to a row of abandoned buildings that fronted the narrow street. At Church Alley two men reached out, covered her head with a hood, and pulled her back into the darkness. She swung the metal case around and struck both men, one on the shoulder, a glancing blow, and the other man in the face; the metal cut his cheek to the bone. Felipa recovered hours later; she was tied to the pipes in a cold and dark room in a building near the church and the statue of Pocahontas.

Miigis dreamed an earlier season over the thin rose shadows at dawn; she counted the crows in the tender birch. She could hear them, but she could not reach the vast number that bounced and croaked near the trailer house; she could not reach the stories of the crows. Admire licked her hands and barked at the morning star, a blue radiance in the window.

Stone waited that morning for Felipa to telephone as she had promised before she left London. Later he called the Belle Sauvage Inn and learned from the desk clerk that "Madame Flowers has not yet returned to check out." The operator searched the directories, and at last he placed a call to the book collector Pellegrine Treves.

"Felipa has not returned to the hotel," shouted Stone.

"Who might this be?" asked Treves.

"Stone Columbus."

"Yes, forgive me, but we parted before dinner," said Treves.

"Where did she go from the Three Daws?" asked Stone.

"St. George's Parish."

"When did you see her last?"

"As she came out of the church," said Treves.

"Call me if you hear anything," he said, and slammed the receiver down. Stone stood at the window with Miigis and Admire. They could do nothing but wait for the telephone to ring.

Later in the morning a man telephoned and said in a disguised voice that "Felipa Flowers will be released unharmed when you trade the remains of Columbus for Pocahontas."

"Name the place," shouted Stone.

"Gatwick airport in London."

"I don't have a passport," said Stone.

"Boston International, then," said the man.

"When?" asked Stone.

"Tomorrow at midnight."

"Where is she now, put her on the phone," he shouted, but there was silence and then the connection was dead. Stone summoned the heirs to the stone tavern. Christopher Columbus was disinterred once more in the politics of racial terrorism and the shame of colonial fortunes.

Stone was instructed to place the silver casket in a duffel and wait near the curb in front of the departure terminal at Northwest Airlines. The heirs decided that he should travel with Miigis to Boston. He made reservations, packed the purple duffel, the one Felipa carried to New York, and drove to the airport in Minneapolis.

Miigis was awakened by jackdaws in a dream early the next morning, a presentiment. The jackdaws landed on a statue. An hour before their flight was scheduled to depart they learned that Felipa had been found dead in England.

116

Stone drove back to the headwaters in silence. Pellegrine Treves was the first to telephone with the morbid details of her death. Felipa, he said in a broken voice, was found in the morning at the base of the statue of Pocahontas at St. George's Parish Church in Gravesend.

"The cause of death has not been determined, but police have ruled the case a possible murder and have ordered an investigation," said Treves.

"Please, would you search at Gravesend?" asked Stone.

"I understand, say no more," he said, and drove to the church the next morning. He remembered their conversations, the moment she pushed the parish door open, and later, from a distance, her shadow near the statue.

Treves reported to Stone that Felipa was found with her back on the base of the statue, facing the river, her arms and legs were folded to the side, and her head was bent forward on her chest.

Felipa was found with no shoes; her blue moccasins and her leather purse were never located. The metal case had vanished, and was never mentioned to the police or the vicar of the parish. The ladies in the church remembered a late tourist, nothing more.

"I found faint marks in the grass and believe that she was dragged to the statue by two people from the street behind the church," said Treves. "She mentioned white pine that night at the masque, and there was such a cutting at the entrance to an abandoned building across from the church."

Scotland Yard homicide inspectors held the body for two weeks to schedule sophisticated forensic tests and studies to determine the cause of death; however, in the end the case was closed. There was no evidence of alcohol, barbiturates, alkaloids, or any other toxic chemicals in her body fluids or tissue; there were minor bruises on her shoulders, and more serious bruises and contusions on her wrists, but no evidence of mortal wounds or asphyxiation. The cause of death was ruled unintentional, and by natural but unresolved causes. The detective inspectors reported that the deceased, "Felipa Flowers, may have died from exposure or loneliness at Gravesend."

WOODEN HEAD

Harmonia Dewikwe, the government trained manicurist, was saved at last by her own hard head. She was pressed by a monotonous hollow caw to be healed at the new tribal nation announced on talk radio; thereupon she paddled an aluminum canoe into the Strait of Georgia and was overturned in rough seas near Point Assinika.

"She washed up on shore with a waterlogged head near the Trickster of Liberty," roared the pale man with no name. "That very wooden head she came to have healed in the new nation saved her other endowed parts."

The no name man, who would answer to nonce words on occasion, was a pale weaver with a doctorate in consciousness studies from the University of California. He moved to the outback on the reservation and remained a lover and weaver in silence for seven years. The secretive weaver was the third and last man who lived with Binn Columbus.

Now the pale weaver roars the same stories over and over, such as the tale of the woman with the wooden head, and other stories on women; the same stories with new scenes, the seascapes of a new nation. He is bent to recover the silence in turns on a creation theme. That roar at the marina tavern is the common father of Stone Columbus.

"Harmonia lost her original head to the wiindigoo one night as she did his cold nails, so the best head and shoulders shaman of the tribe imagined a new one," he roared near the back of the new tavern on the Miigis Marina. "The manicurist lost two more, so the shaman gave her a wooden head with the mind of a crow, but she hated the croaks and caws, and the black roads in memories, so she headed for the point in a canoe to celebrate the creation of the new tribal nation."

Point Assinika was declared a sovereign nation on October 12, 1992, by the Heirs of Christopher Columbus. "At dawn we saw pale naked people, and we went ashore in the ship's boat," said the adventurer on an exclusive talk show radio broadcast. "Miigis unfurled the royal banner, and the heirs brought the flags which displayed a large blue bear paw.

"The Heirs of Columbus bear faith and witness that we have taken possession of this point in the name of our genes and the wild tricksters of liberties, and we made all the necessary declarations and had these testimonies recorded by a blond anthropologist.

"No sooner had we concluded the formalities of taking possession of the point than people began to come to the beach, all as pale as their mothers bore them, and the women also, although we did not see more than one very young girl," said Stone Columbus on Carp Radio.

Admiral Luckie White, heads of state, tribal leaders, ambassadors, ministers, corporate directors, and those so eager to be healed were there that warm morning to honor the first nation in the histories of the modern world dedicated to protean humor and the genes that would heal.

Point Assinika, otherwise named Point Roberts, situated in the Strait of Georgia between Semiahmoo, Washington, and Vancouver Island, Canada, became the wild estate of tribal memories and the genes of survivance in the New World.

Miigis dreamed the stone tavern at the new tribal nation. She heard the clear voice of her mother once more as a crane on the meadow, and then she dreamed that her mother was a waxwing in the cedar; at last she was with her mother as a water ouzel in the mountains near the peninsula.

Felipa Flowers was buried on the meadow at the House of Life. The Heirs of Columbus continued their stories for several months at the stone tavern to honor her humor and memories, but nothing would ever be the same at the headwaters. Stone waited with Miigis and Admire under the cedar that spring; he fasted and then at last he shouted in seven panic holes on the night of a new moon. The meadow turned a wild herbal blue.

Miigis was silent under the cedar; she never cried, and the birds she dreamed were lonesome. She would mourn until her mother returned as a bird. Admire barked, but she would not whistle until the heirs were at sea once more.

The heirs shouted back, and the mongrels barked to each other in succession. "No one has roared that loud since no name and the founder of the panic holes, Luster Browne, the Baron of Patronia," said Binn Columbus. The meadow burst into bloom that spring, but the crows were mean in the birch, the politicians were obtrusive and bothersome, and treasure hunters roamed in search of the booties of civilization on the meadow and down to the headwaters. Truman shouted at the tribal police to consider the traditions of the heirs, the sacred meadow and the stone tavern, but the reservation politicians would never overcome their envies of the *Santa María Casino*.

"That notorious bingo barge, the disruptions of the sky with lasers, the controversies over the remains of Columbus and Pocahontas, and then the murder of Felipa have brought too much adverse public attention to the reservation," said the otiose tribal attorney.

"You mean the greed of reservation politicians," said Stone.

"No, we mean your crazy notions that the heirs can heal people, and because of that stupid radio show, thousands of sick and deformed white people come to the reservation, and some of them stay, such as your own father," said the lawyer.

The tribal politicians were determined to remove the crossblood heirs as members of the reservation, so they hired a private investigator to report on the wealth, associations, and unusual activities of the Heirs of Columbus. Almost Browne, who had once been banned from the reservation, and his laser light shows continued to be a source of serious shamanic contention. The politics of race were never secure, even less so as the humor and bingo cash returns were envied, but the case of a stone stolen from the tavern late that spring tested the balance of recast traditions, trickster humor, political auguries, and the ovine tribal police.

Truman Columbus reported that a stone had been stolen and croaked that the tribal police would not investigate, "because the stone that heals is the stone that burns." The tribal police captain said that her men were humiliated by the complaint, and to search for a "common stone was stupid at best." The police woman told a newspaper reporter that "stones are not stolen unless stones are owned, and that rock pile on the meadow is tribal trust land, which means that the stones are owned by the tribe, not the Heirs of Columbus."

Stone Columbus told the heirs that the time had come to move closer to the mountains and the ocean. The *Santa María Casino* court decision had inspired his notion of sovereignty. That spring the heirs bought land and hired contractors to build a marina and pavilions on the south shore at Point Roberts, Washington. Then the heirs moved the stone tavern, one stone at a time, and soon the earth was warm and healed at the point.

Stone commissioned the crossblood sculptor Bat Bartholdi to move and complete the enormous crotch high copper statue of the Trickster of Liberty. Ginseng Browne, an heir to the wild baronage on the reservation, was once the world trader of that rare wild ginseng; he negotiated a million dollar trade agreement with the People's Republic of China. The Chinese built the statue to honor their exclusive rights to buy the golden ginseng.

The Trickster of Liberty was crotch high by the time Ginseng Browne was indicted for "rustling an endangered root" and violations of the species treaties. Overnight crows croaked in the cavernous waist of the abandoned statue. The politicians and tribal police danced with the crows when the monster was removed from the reservation.

121

The Trickster of Liberty faced west on the point and would be higher than the Statue of Liberty. The trickster embraced the humor of the tribal world with his head in the clouds. The inscription on the statue promised to "heal the tired tribes and huddled masses yearning to breathe free."

Stone deposited several million dollars in mutual escrow accounts and commissioned an international bank to negotiate conditional contracts to pursue genetic therapies and biogenetic research on survivance to heal the tribal world. Five nations, seventeen companies, three shamans, and several independent scientists responded to the invitation and signed potential agreements to share the discoveries with a new, but unstated, tribal nation and corporation. The heirs would heal with their genetic inheritance and leave the rest to the price wars of the wise and ancient civilizations.

Stone commissioned three ferries for basic transportation and leased several barges at the Port of Seattle. He loaded the barges with scientific instruments and equipment, computers and accessories, generators that would be fueled by methane toilets, pavilions, circus tents, and last but not least the equipage of a new bingo casino. The adventurer had endured his wounds and bereavement; now he was at sea once more in high humor. His ambitious course would heal millions of lonesome and wounded children.

Admiral Luckie White, the radio patron of the heirs, had been invited with several tribal writers, artists, and entertainers to christen the *Santa María Ferry*. "October sunrise over the mountains and paradise in the Port of Seattle," soughed Admiral White.

Miigis hoisted the banner, a blue bear paw on a blood red background with a black spirit catcher on the canton, the colors of the new nation of Point Assinika. Stone saluted, horns blasted, and there were loud cheers on the dock.

Luckie White was pleased and amused to be on the voyage to the new tribal world, but only when the banner was raised, and the ferryboat was under way, did she understand that "wild and marvelous moment of tribal sovereignty." The *Santa María Ferry* was the flagship of the tribal armada; two ferries and seven barges were close behind in Puget Sound.

The *Santa María Ferry* sailed between the San Juan Islands into the Strait of Georgia. Stone was at the bridge dressed in his scarlet tunic. Miigis sounded the horns and waved to the people in the boats that passed the armada. The placards on the sides of the barges, and banners on the ferries, announced the tribal insurrection: "Columbus Takes Back the New World at Point Roberts." Hundreds of pleasure boats, a natural flotilla, followed the ferries to the new marina on the south shore of the point.

Carp Radio was on the air with the first live broadcast of the creation of a tribal nation. Stone Columbus had announced the time and date of the insurrection earlier in the summer, but most people assumed it was part of the quincentenary for Christopher Columbus. Network television scorned the announcement as one of many counterevents of the day, and the heirs were old radio news since the bingo barge sank in a thunderstorm. Corporate advertisers, however, were wiser, and eager to be heard at the same time as Stone Columbus.

"Admiral White is on the air with the truth of the night much earlier than usual so we can bring you the actual creation of a tribal nation as we promised last month on Carp Radio," said Luckie White.

"Stone Columbus and his mariners have anchored the *Santa María Ferry* to the new Miigis Marina, and you can hear the cheers from the hundreds of curious well-wishers on boats near the shore, and now the man who claims he is an heir and the namesake of that great explorer who landed in the New World five hundred years ago today is about to raise their flag and declare, at this very moment, a sovereign nation.

"The Trickster of Liberty, that marvelous copper giant dedicated to tribal humor, was moved from the reservation and now stands on shore near the marina, more than a hundred and eighty feet, head to toe, taller than the Statue of Liberty."

Stone hoisted the red banner with the blue bear paw and shouted into the microphone: "This flag represents our survivance and the sovereignty of Point Assinika." Miigis danced on the blue copper moccasins on the trickster statue. Admire barked under the hollow trickster and then she puckered her blue lips for the first time in several months and whistled a wild tune from the *New World* Symphony, by Dvořák.

The point was claimed by the heirs as a free state with no prisons, no passports, no public schools, no missionaries, no television, and no public taxation; genetic therapies, natural medicine, bingo cards, and entertainment were free to those who came to be healed and those who lived on the point. The residents who owned land on the point were overcome with the humor of the moment; there was no resistance, because there was nothing to lose. Bingo would pay for local services, and games of chance would heal the wounded and the lonesome.

Several government agencies had the heirs, the scientists, and their research under surveillance; state and federal officials were cautious and did not move against the insurrection because of public sympathies raised by radio talk shows. Several national polls indicated that the public was in favor of the new tribal state. That the new nation honored humor and common sense, and was dedicated to heal children without taxation, inspired millions of citizens who contributed more cash to the gene banks than they had ever given in the past to television evangelists. Carp Radio encouraged citizens to open gene banks with their cash in every state to further the research on survivance in the New World.

"Radio is real, and the rest is bad television," said Stone.

"Our listeners are watching," said Luckie White.

"Right, what we hear on radio is what we see, and the remains, mean crows and evangelists, are poses on television," said Stone. The bear paw waved in a light breeze under the crotch of the Trickster of Liberty.

"Stone Columbus, our man of the hour, once more on talk show radio, has come full circle from a sovereign bingo barge to more bingo and a new nation of gene banks," said the Admiral.

"Jesus Christ heals with bingo," shouted Stone.

"Name the winners," said the Admiral.

"Wiindigoo at a moccasin game, Columbus, Pocahontas, Wovoka, Crazy Horse, George Washington, Felipa, my father, and the soldiers of fortune and independence were gamblers, and healers," said Stone.

"Wiindigoo needs a voice for our listeners," said the Admiral.

"That evil gambler was frozen in motion by the ice woman on the last draw with the tribe, now that was a moccasin game, and we were healed, but she holds him in her cave for a future game," said Stone.

Almost Browne created a laser light show that night to commemorate the new nation. Christopher Columbus arose with a burst of light in the east and came ashore; his head swelled and turned blue near the Trickster of Liberty. The adventurer raised a banner in the name of the monarchs, and then waved his sword over his head, the lase of the blade bounced on the black water.

George Washington marched out of the north and met Crazy Horse and Louis Riel over the marina on the point. Almost was cheered when the four laser men, the adventurer, the general, the warrior, the crossblood, and later a lover and princess combined in a blue radiance near the statue.

Almost sounded the wind in the birch, the rush of summer on the meadow at the headwaters, and the music of sandhill cranes. Then, at a distance in the east, two figures seemed to arise from the bay and dance toward the point. The audience on the marina moaned and cried with tender remembrance; the last two images in the night were Pocahontas and Felipa Flowers on each side of the Trickster of Liberty.

"Stone Columbus is here with a new nation to answer your questions and mine, the truth in the night, so you're on the air Oklahoma City," said the radio admiral.

"My grandmother was an Indian, and we were wondering if you could come down here and fix us a new nation, just like the one you did up there," said the woman from Oklahoma City.

"Fix it for what?" asked Stone.

"You got the bingo, and we got taxes," she said.

"The white man's burden, you've got the time and civilization has the taxes, and we got a commercial announcement," said the Admiral. She was silent, listened with her head back, and counted the seconds of a new aspirin advertisement, a precise touch of material time. "Carp Radio is back to take your calls, questions, and comments from listeners around the world."

"Point Assinika is a natural nation," said Stone. "Humor rules and tricksters heal in our state, and we have no checkpoints or passports, no parking meters to ruin the liberty of the day."

"Pocatello, Idaho, you're on the air tonight," said Admiral White.

"Columbus was lost, so what's with you?" asked Pocatello.

"Slowfood, mongrels that whistle, panic hole parks, a statue with a sense of humor, genes that heal, and the most dangerous herb in the history of the world," said Stone.

"What's so special about that?"

"Nothing," said Stone.

"Wait a minute, slow down, you've told us about tribal panic holes, the primal shout that raises gardens, and other incredible things, but what on earth is this bad herb?" asked the Admiral.

"Nothing, we inherited the genes that heal, and dreamed the herb that could eliminate the world, and now we can shout from our own sovereign nation," said Stone.

"Stone, our listeners want the truth at night," said the Admiral.

"The tribal truth is what you hear," said Stone.

"But a killer herb?"

"Yes, the war herb could eliminate humans, time, and civilization, in the right combination the herb causes people to vanish from memory and history," said Stone.

"So, why the secret?" asked Admiral White.

"We never needed the herb before now," said Stone.

"Carp Radio with the incredible truth of the night, and now a public service announcement," said the radio admiral. She counted the seconds and smiled at the same time over the herb revelation. "We're back, and you heard the future here for the first time, the gene man has a secret herbal power, and you're on the air Rapid City."

"Where did you hear that herb?"

"That's a secret, only dreamers can touch this powerful herb, and yet thousands of people have vanished with a mere thought of the herb, and no one ever knew why," said Stone.

126

"Black Elk had a vision of a war herb that was so powerful it could destroy the white man, but he was a man of peace and never told how to find it," said Rapid City.

"Black Elk was a dreamer," said Stone.

"So, how do you know about this war herb?" asked the radio admiral. "Who told you the stories, and what are you going to do with the war herb?"

"Binn Columbus heard the herb," said Stone.

"Come on, touch me with your wild herb, give me your best shot in the dark," said Luckie White. "Let's see who's eliminated on talk show radio in the herb wars, come on with the herbs and our listeners will be the judge."

Admiral White turned to an advertisement and burst into laughter. She broadcast several announcements to enhance the moment, and then with no explanation she was back on the air; the listeners heard the sound of water on the shore near the marina, now and then a voice in the distance, a horn at sea. She teased with silence.

"The Admiral of Carp Radio has returned from the herb wars with a vision," she said in a blithe tone of voice. "The rest of the night holds the truth of our time, and you're on the air Duck Lake, Saskatchewan."

"Stone has been compared to Louis Riel because both of them are crossbloods and leaders of insurrections, and both of their fathers were wool weavers," said Duck Lake.

"Christopher Columbus was raised by a weaver too, so now we have the sons of three weavers, and three explorers in the New World, what's your question?" asked Luckie White.

"Riel was executed for treason," said Duck Lake.

"That's not a question," said the Admiral.

"Riel was a dreamer with too much religion, he was a tragic hero in the blood, but the heirs are comic, we got humor, bingo, and great genes," said Stone.

"Your genes could be the new treason," said Duck Lake.

"Who are you?" asked the radio admiral.

"Louis Riel was my distant relative," said Duck Lake.

"Crossbloods are serious," said Stone.

"Serious about genes?" asked Duck Lake.

"The genes that heal," said Stone.

"Columbus could forgive but never heal your enemies."

"Point Assinika is not our Fort Garry, and besides, Louis Riel never had panic holes to shout into or bingo to prove he was real and sane," said Stone.

"The Heirs of Columbus shout, laugh, and pray to get their way in the New World, but the heirs are closer to creation in their humor than simple confessions, so that's what cut the ice in their insurrection," said the radio admiral. She broadcast a commercial for a sodium free antacid.

"Carp Radio is back with Stone Columbus, the gene man of the New World, and bingo of the night, the heir of the primal hand talkers from the civilization of the Maya to Point Assinika," said Admiral White.

"Columbus landed twice in five centuries," said Stone.

"Indeed he did," said the Admiral.

"Columbus and Jesus are hand talkers," said Stone.

"Albuquerque, what's on your mind tonight?"

"Mayan hand talkers, man you must be crazy."

"Saint Louis, go ahead with your question," said the Admiral.

"How can you tell when you got the right genes?"

"Columbus genes are a signature, we got the chemical code that proves we are the tribal descendants of the great explorer, we got the secret in the stone," said Stone.

"You told, so how can it be a secret?"

"The seventeen gene signature is a tribal secret, and that secret is held in the stone, but soon you might hear about the power of our healer genes," said Stone.

"Admiral Luckie White has the last word, and the last word tonight is in the stone," she said. "Carp Radio has run the wire once more, hear you real soon with your late night voices of the truth."

Luckie White was more amative and custodial as the ratings of her talk show rose higher; over the months with the heirs she had become even more considerate of tribal memories, a radio patron of the heirs and their true adventures. She argued with the station owners that tribal humor was good business, and healed, the new commercials would prove that point; she praised the heirs for not being corrupted by their considerable cash and public attention, or ruined by political censure on the reservation.

GENOME PAVILION

The *New York Times* reported in an editorial that television stations and the federal government have remained silent on the recent insurrection at Point Roberts by the Heirs of Columbus. The report speculated that the silence could be in response to the acquiescence of the residents on the point, the censure of the heirs and crossbloods by tribal governments, but the most obvious consideration was the public support in discussions of the new nation on Carp Radio.

"The White House observed silence on the insurrection, the president was more concerned with television than radio, a doubtable democratic simulation; consequently, the nation would be governed by listeners on late night radio," the editorial reported. "The Heirs of Christopher Columbus are unconcerned over the silence, and the rumors that military units have been activated in the area. That the heirs would give their very genes to save the world is neither ironic nor moronic, as they believe their unique genes are healers. Such noble ambitions, however, are not without critics. Leading scientists are skeptical, to put it kindly, that a ragtag group of rebellious, uneducated mixedbloods would be the actual selective heirs of a 'genetic signature' from Christopher Columbus.

"Doctor Canon Simpson, the outspoken biogenetic engineer, national science adviser, and friend of the president, pointed out that the study of 'genetic inheritance is more than counting the spots on mongrels.'

"Stone Columbus, the tribal bingo tycoon and heirship leader of the insurrection, which has been compared to the métis rebellion of Louis Riel in Canada, told the chairman of the quincentenary commission that 'Columbus would return just as we have, and what was good enough for him is even better for his tribal heirs.' The chairman denied reports that the commission had funded the heirs and the insurrection as a part of quincentenary celebrations. Riel was convicted of treason and hanged in 1885."

The Felipa Flowers Casino was established on the international border between Canada and Point Assinika. Bingo gamblers could enter the bright, enormous tandem pavilions and leave from either nation, as there were no inspections at the tribal border; indeed, the heirs honored tribal identities but no political boundaries on the earth.

Stone never owned a passport, and he would never hold a mere photograph, a political simulation with a national seal, to be more real than the human it represented. "People have died defending the simulations of families in photographs, the loneliness of civilization," he said. Stone has no photographs of Felipa or Miigis; he dreams and remembers them in stories. Miigis remembers her mother as a bird in dreams.

The casino was managed by the pale man with no name; he counted the cash, paid salaries, hired and retired, recorded the presence of enemies and conspirators. There were tribal fascists who would abolish the heirs, their bingo, humor, and certain words, such as *crossblood*, and the genes of survivance; there were government agents and investigators who would overturn the new nation. No name was a controversial overseer, to be sure; he posted "not wanted portraits" of the fascists, investigators, and agents provocateurs, with embellished features, at the entrances to the casino.

Even more unusual was his order that the male casino attendants must crossdress. "Regrettably men are no longer that interesting unless they dress as women," said the father of Stone

131

Columbus. Pale no name was a transvestite, a posture that had no name or instance on the reservation, but the poseur enlivened the casino and was lauded by the patrons. No name, the paramount transvestite, posed as first ladies, either Eleanor Roosevelt, Nancy Reagan, or his favorite, Lady Bird Johnson.

Pavilion communities were established between panic hole parks on the point. The residence and shelter pavilions were located on the rise, protected by a natural stand of hemlock and spruce. The scientific pavilions were laced, one to the other, near the statue and marina. The sides of the blue pavilions were radiant at night, and the massive computers hummed and sounded the beats of memories, the genetic signatures of survivance.

The Dorado Genome Pavilion, the heart of the genetic research, was directed by Doctor Pir Cantrip, an exobiologist turned genetic engineer. He and other scientists had isolated the genetic code of tribal survivance and radiance, that native signature of seventeen mitochondrial genes that could reverse human mutations, nurture shamanic resurrection, heal wounded children, and incite parthenogenesis in separatist women.

The *Ojibwe News* reported that the signature was an "estate antidote to terminal blood quantum creeds." The actuation of parthenogenesis, however, would become the most contestable revision of the signature, the monopolitical reproduction of humans without men.

Molecular biologists and genetic engineers representing five countries rushed to the new tribal nation in search of a place to conduct their genetic research and experiments without state or federal restrictions. The research on polymerase chain reaction in gene copies, genetic therapies, intron, and intromission, for instance, was unwarrantable and banned in most nations to protect the interests of major pharmaceutical companies. Thousands of wounded children would be humored, honored, and healed at Point Assinika.

Doctor Cantrip and his research team had discovered that there were seventeen genes in the signature of survivance; the heirs, shamans, and healers carried an unbroken radiance, a genetic chain from the first hand talkers of creation. Millions of these genetic signatures were copied in vacuum clean laboratories.

"This signature is neither neoteric nor fortuitous, as the genes are a tribal code inherited from hand talkers over five thousand generations," said the genetic engineer. Cantrip had been asked by the State Department to discuss his genetic research with a foursome of molecular biologists from the Soviet Union, and two biorobotic engineers from Japan.

The heirs were certain that the scientists were being used by federal agents as a cover; the genes of survivance and resurrection had never been a secret, but the overt and noticeable inheritance must be driven covert to have value as agency intelligence. The agents, cozen in their best suits, were determined not to have their portraits mounted at the casino.

Stone demanded copies of the identification cards of the agents from the State Department; he told them that "temporary visas were required of those who posed as intelligence agents." The agents loosened their ties and denied their covert identities.

"Listen, the genes have been around since stones and snow crystals, nothing new here, but that herb is our real secret," said Stone. The agents would not believe what he told them until a military satellite detected a radiant shadow or hot spot at Point Assinika. That most secret intelligence was overheard, and in less than a week there were special representatives at the point from the Soviet Union, France, Japan, Israel, Iraq, Libya, the Navaho Nation, and the People's Republic of China. The Chinese reminded the heirs of their earlier trade in ginseng, the Soviet Union praised their tribal cultures, the French could not avoid their memorable arrogance in the fur trade, and more; each nation pursued an accordance over the war herb, and promised to support the nomination of Point Assinika in the United Nations.

Cantrip never seemed to be overcome by political intrigues; he was in his seventies, thin at the neck and thick at the waist, mannered and manicured, and he bore the constant scent of sardines. Pir, a recent émigré, was secretive about his past, as if he had a past to hide. The heirs were pleased with his dedication and scientific credentials; the recognition of his peers; his praise of shamans, hand talkers, and their stories; and his true mind to heal children, those who were the lonesome mutants of a chemical civilization.

Cantrip insisted that the heirs listen to what scientists and other visitors were told about the genetic research in the Dorado Genome Pavilion. The heirs and shamans were eager to hear about their inheritance; as a consequence, the scientific information on tours was both essential and theoretical. Miigis, Gracioso, Memphis, Truman, and no name in basic black were on the lecture tour that morning with the scientists and agents from the State Department.

"There are, as you know, four crucial substances, adenine, cytosine, guanine, and thymine, in a deoxyribonucleic acid molecule, and three billion codes and signatures," said Pir Cantrip. "These four letters are held together in a signature by their opposites, the biochemical codes are bound by their own opposition, and here is where the shaman and the trickster touch that primal source of humor, imagination, and the stories that heal right in the antinomies of the genetic code," he said. Pir was nervous on tours and his voice wavered.

Cantrip motioned with his hands for the heirs and others to gather at several computer monitors. Blue stars bounced into snow crystals, and hand talkers were created in a simulation. "The opposite has no power without the other, as a woman would resist a man, the wise one must be a moron to survive, and the chemicals of genes can be touched in meditation and memories, that blue radiance is a wondrous instance in human creation, and those who can imagine their antinomies and mutations are able to heal with humor."

"Mongrels hear the blue," said Gracioso.

"The trickster is a mutation of their creation," said Cantrip.

"Mongrels imagined humans," said Gracioso.

"I dream my mother as a bird," said Miigis.

"Doctor Cantrip, would you review your scientific methods and explain why you considered mitochondrial genetic research, which depends, as it does, on a mother?" said a scientist from the Soviet Union.

"We use enzymes to fragment the molecule, and then, in a synthetic substance, the pieces are touched with electrical current," said Cantrip. "This basic procedure is called electrophoresis, and then the nucleotide fragments are separated and treated with a radioactive material so they can be seen, of course, and the result of this is our genetic signature."

"Do acausal genes form the sequences?" asked a scientist.

"My genes are personal," said Memphis.

"We compare these basic signatures that would establish a structure, or generative grammar, as it were, to estimate and measure the radiometric mutations, the obvious comparison, one animal to the other, and then the genetic codes are copied."

"Mongrels and humans once more," said Gracioso.

"Precisely, we can determine by computer simulations and comparison the permutations of a signature of humans and other genetic memories," said Cantrip.

"Would there be resurrection genes?" asked an agent.

"Stone Columbus is the paragon of resurrections, and, as you know, genetic signatures do not exist in isolation, you might say that genes are the everlasting opposition in communal imagination, ironies, and memories, the very energies and agonistic humor of tricksters and shamans," said Cantrip.

"Columbus is the basic signature," said an agent.

"Christopher Columbus has the same genetic signature of survivance, we have concluded from laboratory and computer studies, as the hand talkers and his namesake five centuries later," said Cantrip.

"Can you prove that?" asked a woman from the Soviet Union.

"Naturally, the seventeen gene signature is the same in both men," said Cantrip. "Stone, his genetic signature, was determined by molecular genetic analysis, and Christopher Columbus carried the same signature that was confirmed in several reliable studies of his bones and dried blood on a lead ball found at the bottom of his casket."

"The sequences are the same?"

"Yes, there is no sequence divergence in the seventeen gene signature of the mitochondrial material, and we are secure that our studies of nuclear DNA confirm the signature," said Cantrip.

"What about the research on the genome narratives?"

"The genome narratives are stories in the blood, a metaphor for racial memories, or the idea that we inherit the structures of language and genetic memories; however, our computer memories and simulations are not yet powerful enough to support what shamans and hand talkers have inherited and understood for thousands of years," said Cantrip.

"Biogenetic robotics?" asked the scientists from Japan.

"Our research in this critical and controversial area has been more theoretical and computer simulated than genetic intromission, but we are eager to dedicate one of our research pavilions to that end," said Cantrip.

"Robotics is critical to the military," said an agent.

"Naturally, imagine a biogenetic robotic intelligence agent?" Cantrip mentioned *Mind Children*, by Hans Moravec, and then told the agent that "future generations of 'human beings could be designed by mathematics, computer simulations' as robots are now, and a 'mix of fabulous substances, including, where appropriate, living biological materials' that would be superhuman, leaving human agents as second rate, not to mention those in intelligence."

Memphis purred near the computers.

Cantrip folded his hands on his chest and bowed to the heirs and the scientists. "That concludes our tour and the introduction to our research here at Point Assinika." He bowed a second time.

"You have been very generous," said a Soviet.

"However, before you leave our new nation, we insist that you accept our invitation to a special luncheon, a certified manicure, and a card or two of bingo at our new Felipa Flowers Casino," said Cantrip.

The first ladies transvestite moved so close to a robotics scientist that he trembled and wetted his cheeks with sweat. Gracioso pursued the two agents with stories about mongrels in the cold war and oxymora in greeting cards and military intelligence. Memphis purred louder behind the two men from the Soviet Union. The panther touched their shoulders with her paws, and the scientists shuddered.

Memphis purred in wild overtones as the team of scientists wandered through the hemlock to the casino. The scientists were bothered by their fear of animals, even more because they were in a tribal nation. One woman scientist was moved to confess her fear of animals to a panther and a mongrel. Memphis said, "You are a nation of bears, you must be brave." Gracioso invited her to visit the mongrels at the residence pavilions to balance her fear of animals, but she was soothed by the music in the casino and the humor of the manicurists.

The Felipa Flowers Casino has been crowded with gamblers from the minute the pavilion opened, day and night. Bingomania had matured as a new human condition of racial associations over the remains of civilization. The first lady with no name was now dressed as Lady Bird Johnson. She encouraged much humor in the casino, and no name even trained several mongrels to cross-dress and howl wingo, wingo, wingo, when a winner would shout bingo.

Harmonia Dewikwe, the manicurist with the wooden head, named the transvestite the wingo man, and mocked his manners, poses, and wild laughter as the first ladies of the casino and the new nation.

MUTE CHILD

Teets Melanos saw the mute child come out of the hemlock with two blue puppets. The manicurist, who had earned a venerable tribal seal for her dedication to hands, told the heirs that there were other children on the cold wisps of winter that night. She envisioned the blues who had landed in the rain at Point Assinika.

The child, a hand talker with blue hands, entered the casino that night on the first new moon of the year. The casino was crowded as usual with wounded gamblers, and others from communities close to the border. The aisles were boisterous carnivals to the bone; even so, the mere presence of the child, and the wild chatter of his puppets, caused waves of silence to reach the center of the storm. The sounds of numbers wavered, machines were hushed, and players turned in their chairs to see the blue traces of the child in the pavilion. The silence was spontaneous and spiritual; the child was honored with silence.

The luminous child circled the bingo tables in the center of the casino and then, at the back near the restaurant and concessions, he pushed open the padded double doors to the Parthenos Manicure Salon. The trace of his hands rested on the red doors, and his blue course continued in the casino.

Teets heard the doors swing open behind the manicure chairs as she trimmed the nails of an older woman; later she would remember the unusual silence in the casino, but thought nothing of it at the time. The child smiled and moved closer; not even the chatter of the puppets distracted her attention to fingernails.

Teets concentrated on the cuticle, a handmaiden at the push of the orangewood; she sensed his presence, but she was not aware of the child until the manicure table and their hands turned blue. The woman was breathless that her time had come in a blue light, but then she saw the bright child with the puppets, not the beacon of death. The blue radiance seemed to be natural in the salon, as it had been to the gamblers who had never seen a hand talker before, as natural as death, and no one responded with fear; so natural that the manicurist never wondered how such a luminous child could survive the cold weather, or the cruelties of the modern world. Even more wondrous were the little blues outside at the windows of the casino.

Chilam Balam was his tribal name, the heirs learned later, but Teets and Harmonia named the child Blue Ishi, the last survivor of the mountain hand talkers. Chilam had sailed to the point with the secret tribe of little people, the miniature blues who once lived near the Klinaklini River and Mount Waddington in the Coastal Mountains of western British Columbia.

Chilam was bright and silent, the blue puppets chattered, and the little blues bounced outside in the storm. The gamblers were charmed by the luminous child, and haunted at the same time by the remote blue smiles of the little people at the windows. The manicurists, on the other hand, were awed by the blues, and could not understand how such a curious tribe remained undiscovered in the mountains. That night their stories would be remembered in the blood.

"My grandmother told me about the blues," said Harmonia.

"The blues are fireflies," said Miigis.

"I have been waiting all my life for my blue child to come back home, at last, this must be my second coming," she said. Teets dreamed that she was a blue child at sea with natural ears and a regenerated mouth, a hand talker in the blood. There were no separations in her dreams.

"To the manner born," said Eleanor Roosevelt.

"Thank God this child didn't show up on Christmas Eve, right in the middle of the cross card, because someone would have shouted, and the second coming would have been a wingo," said Harmonia.

Blue Ishi climbed into the padded manicure chair and held his hands out, as the breathless woman had done. His nails were blue, a lighter hue than his blue hands. The radiance of his hands shimmered on the stainless steel counter; the blue was more than mere light, more than a shine, a tribal cache, or luster in a scene; the blue that traced his touch and hovered in silence was the lambent animation of memories that healed.

"This kid's a living flashlight," said the first lady.

"If he's a flashlight then you're a burned out bulb, mister wingo, that's no common beam, he's got the blue power of creation in case you didn't notice," said the manicurist with the wooden head. Harmonia would never own a word that came from the man with no name; she was dissentious no matter the stories he told at night. She dreamed that her wooden head became real on a warm blue wave.

Teets and Harmonia, the casino manicurists, were hesitant at first to touch the child; they had trimmed the nails on more than a thousand hands each over the years to earn their tribal seals of eminence, but they had never seen natural blue nails, but on the dead, and would never understand his blue touch, or the natural course of his hands in creation.

Stone told the manicurists that some dreams were primal memories, others were separations, mythic resolutions, and the blues were stories heard in the blood, the sources of tribal realities and consciousness.

Chilam turned his head and the afterimage was blue in the chair; he touched the manicurists and their hands were blue, a thermoluminescence was created on his breath, in his touch, and silent presence.

Teets Melanos had the most handsome hands in the tribal world; the ancestors posed in the thin bones, as lean and clean as raccoons, but she was chastened and subdued by her enormous head, twisted mouth and smile, close eyes, and her wild ears were creased and shriveled. Two birds were tattooed on her breasts to capture the gaze of men, but she was abused, and she was taunted by children. The heirs heard a tender soul and a lonesome woman; she might have been a teacher, but now she hums and trims, hums and polishes with tribal eminence.

Teets was trusted as a tribal manicurist to hear the secrets of women and the concessions of men, more than a shaman or a priest would hear on the reservation; she became the trusted listener at the casino. Over and over she heard the stories from women and children about abusive men, stories that would alter and attune the tribal world.

Stone had invited her to treat hands at the *Santa María Casino* on Lake of the Woods, and in the course of her manicures, the heirs discovered a discrete method of gathering genetic material and genealogical stories on tribal members. He promised that she would be the first to receive a genetic implant; she was inspired that her head and mouth would be regenerated by the genes of the heirs, the signature of survivance.

Teets amassed thousands of secret bits of skin and fingernail from the hands she manicured. The samples and genealogies provided molecular biologists with the genetic material they needed to isolate and compare the signature of survivance borne by the Heirs of Columbus. The bits and stories would be the source of genetic intromission and retral transformations at the Dorado Genome Pavilion.

The manicurist imagined that she could unite women and men with their nails and cuticles; a return to the stories in the blood, their tricksters in the stone, the fires in the eye and hand roused from crystal and the mire in cold water. She selected bits of fingernails and skin and tumbled them in olive jars, a wild and peculiar ritual. She possessed hundreds of tumbled identities under glass on shelves in the salon. The wind and the breath of bears were moments of portentous conceptions on the nights she tumbled the jars. She was convinced that the heirs had created the blue child in the hemlock to heal women.

141

Binn Columbus never had a manicure, but now and then that winter she sat in the salon and listened to the voices in the jars; alas, she heard her lover, the weaver and first lady who was held as a prisoner by hundreds of women, "and they turned him into a crossdresser and slave."

Harmonia Dewikwe pretended to hear the same voices of the women, but from another source; she had learned from radical feminists on the reservation that the first lady had once been a professor of consciousness studies, not a student as he allowed the tribe to believe, and because of his notorious record of sexual harassment on the campus he was captured and held for more than a year as a slave.

"Mister wingo had two dicks in his head, named his first ladies, and they competed with each other for control of his mouth and hands, so you might say he was always giving someone a piece of his mind," said Harmonia.

"Whatever could you mean?" mocked Teets.

"The first ladies were ever erect in the sixties and never matured, so he ended up teaching to ease his mind, and he eased it so much that more than a hundred women complained that he traded grades for sexual favors," said Harmonia.

"He was much better as a silent weaver," said Binn.

"The women caught the professor in the act, marched him into a cave in the woods behind the university, lashed him to a tree with his underpants down, tied fresh meat to his pink dick, and when the animals came to feed, he screamed and promised to crossdress and weave, mend, and cook for the women, if they would save his dick," said Harmonia.

Binn and the two manicurists laughed so hard they cried in their chairs. Once more the women of the new nation told stories about men, the stories of mischance, with a touch of pure vengeance, that would liberate the cade humor of the trickster and heal the mind.

"The first ladies proved there's no such thing as a free lunch with that man, so we just have to figure out how to eat on our own," said Teets.

"What else you got in those jars?" asked Binn.

142

"I got some skin and a bit of blue fingernail from that sweet child, but who could we tumble with him?" asked Teets. "We might hear nothing but silence."

"Miigis, now that would be some tumble," said Harmonia.

"Not my granddaughter, she's a dream bird," said Binn.

"Perfect, a bird and a blue mute," said Teets.

"Give me a listen," she said at last. Binn turned the jar with care, as if her granddaughter were inside, and the jar turned blue; the sides were warm, and when she opened the jar blue fireflies lighted the salon. She heard birds, wisps of music, the wind, nothing more.

Miigis encountered Chilam Balam and the fireflies later in the Dorado Genome Pavilion. The mute child and the blues becalmed humans, hushed their machines, beset the scientists and brave mongrels, and stimulated the radiometers and sensitive instruments.

Pir Cantrip, and the scientists from other nations, were surrounded by blues in their laboratories. The little people touched their hands and turned them blue. Pir, however, held back; his hands were blotched, viridescent, and he moaned, a black currish wail from the shadows of his troubled soul. The blues teased a demon in the scientist; evil memories lurked behind his nervous tongue.

Miigis heard her dream bodies with the mute child and the blues; she learned how to see the traces of creation in memories; the blue afterimages of leaves, the breath of animals, the aura of humans, the blue seams and tiers of stories in the blood and stone.

Point Assinika announced that the lonesome and wounded would be healed with dreams, blue memories, and the signature of survivance; those who heard the stories on late night talk radio sailed, drove, and hitchhiked by the hundreds to be humored in the blood at the pavilions. The wounded who waited to be healed and regenerated were given free meals, bingo cards, and hand care in the Parthenos Manicure Salon.

The genes healed the lonesome, to be sure, and most of those who were wounded and deformed at birth, or by accident, but not everyone heard the bodies they had seen in dreams. The heirs and the blues were masters of the energies that healed and regenerated lost limbs, the crushed, tormented, and those who were misconceived in wicked storms.

Pir had developed the in vivo genetic therapies of survivance, the implanted genes of the heirs, but only shamans and tricksters were able to stimulate the trickster opposition in the genes, the ecstatic instructions, and humor in the blood. The scientists delivered the genetic signatures, the tribal healers touched the wounded and heard their creation stories.

Teets and Harmonia waited with the wounded children to derive the genes and dream their bodies with the blues. The new moieties to heal were the genes of survivance and stories in the blood.

Point Assinika was the first crossblood nation dedicated to heal the wounded with genetic therapies; the genes were implanted, but the children need more than genetic codes, more than protein stimulation; the heirs were overclouded by thousands of children with genetic diseases, more than they could touch with stories and humor. Chilam and the blues came at the right time to heal; the point was the last tribal nation in the world that would honor their dream bodies and blue touch of creation.

Padrino de Torres had not been lonesome in the world since he had renounced the racialism of the church, the disconsolate nights as a priest, and decided to abide with the humor of abandoned, broken, and wounded tribal children.

Padrino heard about the creation of the nation, as so many others had, on talk radio; a few weeks later he was on the road with several hundred tribal children in school buses bound for the nation that healed. More and more wounded children followed on buses from western reservations and cities. The buses and children were turned back at the border between Canada and the United States. Tribal people were not allowed to cross the international border on their way to Point Assinika.

The children would not be denied their dream to be healed; no matter the cold wet weather, their wounds and disabilities, several hundred children marched in silence that night over the border into a wooded area near Boundary Bay. Padrino played his guitar, and the children chanted as they marched, "Jesus our Maya, be our shaman on this broken night, heal the dreamers with your blue touch, our stories in the blood."

The Felipa Flowers Casino appeared in the distance to be a carnival; the children came upon the bright pavilions with delight. The mongrels barked at the border and then panted when they saw the tribal children, and so many of them to nose. Admire touched the little ones, and then licked them with her blue tongue.

Padrino and three scouts heard the shouts over bingo in the pavilions, not the first sounds they expected to hear at the new nation. He opened the door of the casino, and several hundred children followed him single file into the pavilion. The tribal children hobbled and limped, some without legs, others without arms, and many who were blind, but no one seemed to notice, because most of the gamblers in the casino were wounded, deformed, and grotesque. The children caught the scent of fast food and rushed to the concessions counter at the back of the pavilion.

"My friends want hotdogs," said a blind child.

"How many?" asked the waiter. Caliban, the heir and great white mongrel, amused the children as a waiter. He wore brocaded velvet and a wide elaborate lace collar, and pretended to be Pocahontas in London.

"Well, several hundred," said Padrino.

"What would you like on them?"

"Well, mustard, and relish, but how much?" asked Padrino.

"As much as you want," said Caliban.

"I mean the cost," said Padrino.

"Wait a minute," he said, and laughed.

"You must be here for the genes, right?" asked the first lady.

"Yes, we've been on the road for weeks," said Padrino.

"Food, the genes, everything is free," said the first lady.

"You look very familiar to me," said Padrino. He studied her face, but could not remember a name or place. "Please, have we met somewhere?"

"At the White House?"

"No, not me, never been there," said Padrino.

"My husband was the president."

145

"Please forgive me," said Padrino.

"Lady Bird, Lady Bird," shouted a child.

"You can never be sure of what you see," said the first lady as she patted the heads of the children at the concession. "What's that saying, play bingo and the world comes to your numbers?"

Padrino saw the trace of a beard, unusual gestures, and realized at last that the first lady was a crossdresser. He was not surprised because he had known several priests who were so lonesome they dressed as women to prepare their meals.

The children ate sweet macaroni and cheese, hotdogs, and glorified wild rice, and laughed when the mongrels howled wingo; later some of the children played bingo, others watched television movies, and a few visited the Parthenos Manicure Salon.

Teets was moved by the children; she washed their hands, cleaned and trimmed their fingernails. As she polished and painted their nails the children told her stories about their wounds, tribal demons, the abuses of men on the reservation, and the lonesome nights and humiliations over their bodies. They dreamed new bodies and came to the point, the last place on the earth that would heal their wounds with no conditions.

"Men, men, wicked men," chanted Harmonia.

"So many wounds to heal in the world," said Teets.

"That's why we're here, to manicure the hands of women and children, those wounded by men," she said. Harmonia argued for separatism that night, for a pavilion that healed women, but she was reminded that the heirs and the new nation were the tribal cure, not the cause of wounded women. Stories, she was told, were better to heal, even to hate, than to separate. "Even so," she insisted, "we have a right to our own stories in the blood, and without men."

Chilam and Miigis dreamed their blue bodies with the children, and the blues touched them with humor; the scientists implanted the genes of the heirs, the signature that healed their wounds and regenerated their bodies. The children became their dreams, the memories their bodies carried from the stone.

146

Luckie White announced on radio that hundreds of children, "shunned in an unforgiven material world, threw down their crutches and came out of that wacky gene casino on the run, tribal children were reborn with the genes of survivors and the touch of little blue people, hand talkers and such, and somehow this thing works, just listening to the stories, and watching this thing develop as a science, has changed me over the past year."

The announcement on late night talk radio was an invitation to more and more wounded children, thousands of mutants poisoned in a chemical civilization, and those with unforgiven cancers, plastic faces, wooden hearts, heads, broken tribal minds and dreams; thousands of wounded children arrived at the point by land, sea, and on foot over the border. Thousands and thousands of abandoned and abused children came to the new nation on their last dreams to be healed with the humor of their ancestors in the stone, the protean trickster, the visions of shamans, and the Heirs of Christopher Columbus.

Saint Louis Bearheart, the crossblood of the tribal apocalypse, wrote in his novel *The Heirship Chronicles* that children wore plastic faces at the end of civilization, molded pouts and smiles, to cover cancers; their faces had been "eaten by poison rain." The masks were clear torsions. "Muscles and flesh twitched and quivered behind the plastic; stained teeth were exposed like those of hideous skeletons." The children tried to whisper with no lips, "hlastic haces."

Padrino de Torres, and several children in that first wave to be healed, remained on the point to work in the casino and to help the other children who were landing by the thousands.

Teets and her birds were admired by the former priest. She watched him prepare children to be healed with their fingernails in perfect condition; he was the best man she could not resist. Padrino was convinced by practice that manicures were suitable for children, they were transformed; the close attention to their nails liberated their stories. He would become a manicurist dedicated to the hands of children.

Luckie White was at the casino and pavilions more and more, and less and less as the host of late night talk radio; she had come to the nation with primal dreams of the hand talkers, and to be closer to Miigis and Stone.

"Luckie is a nickname that was once retained in our synagogues as mazeltov, an expression of good luck, to be lucky," said Luckie White. "You see, my relatives were hand talkers, Sephardic Jews."

Mazeltov had talked the nation out of television, passive simulations, and back to the imagination of late night radio; she convinced the listeners to support the resurrection of the new tribal nation, the blue healers, and the Heirs of Christopher Columbus.

Meanwhile, the women in the casino were persuaded by the first lady and the manicurists to establish a nation that would heal women and direct scientific research on the genetic signature of parthenogenesis.

The scientists from other nations, eager to search for genetic cures and therapies, were overcome by the emotional burdens of the wounded tribal children, the abandoned mutants of chemicals; however, the scientists were enticed by the potential fortunes in genetic research on parthenogenesis. Simple genetic intromission conceptions would be worth billions of dollars, a new genetic trope to power in a feminist separatist world.

The Parthenos Manicure Salon became the New World pavilion to heal women, recount the ecstatic creation of children without men or their sperm, and encourage the genetic research on the signature of parthenogenesis. Luckie told the manicurists that she might choose to conceive a good luck child with the ecstasies of dream bodies.

"The Blessed Virgin Mary imagined the child she conceived in a burst of blues, so our annunciation could be the same, clonal imagination and parthenogenesis, or the ecstasies of wild dance, dreams, meditation, or even a big win at bingo," said Luckie White.

"The wingo tribe," shouted Harmonia.

"This is serious, we're talking about perfect children, women without men means more girls than boys in our nation," said Teets. She touched the birds on her breasts.

"Birds of a feather," said the first lady, but the women in the salon moaned the cliché down before he could finish. He paused and tried another idea. "The crossdresser is a painted bird in a borrowed nest."

"Not my birds," said Teets.

"Our Lady of the wingo casino," said Luckie White.

PARTHENOS SALON

Blue Ishi reached into a hemlock to hear their tribal stories; the heart was warm, a sacred hollow in the evergreen. The scientists were enchanted by the blues, and trusted tribal humor as an antidote, but the nation was divided over the sentience of the hemlock and their stories.

Most of the scientists, molecular biologists, genetic engineers, and the others from several nations, were on one side of the issue as rationalists, empiricists, and logical positivists; on the other side of the summit that winter morning at the point were the blues, the wounded, the manicurists, and the Heirs of Columbus.

Pir Cantrip, the first lady, and casino crossdressers were on the line between the blues and the gene men, and negotiated the terms of the wager. Uta Moot, the robotics engineer, did not stand with the other scientists on the issue of arboreal sentience; she was roused by the mute child and pursued the animation of robots that would heal with remembered stories. The first robot at the nation would second the spirit of the evergreens.

"Our play has never been the scientific method, but with the pure pleasure of creation, the blue in the pith, our memories are in the hemlock," said Stone.

"So, what's the bet?" asked Lady Bird Johnson.

"Overnight with that new robot," said Harmonia.

"With the losers?" asked Teets.

"No, no, the winners get the robot," she answered.

"The losers crossdress in the casino overnight," said the first lady. She turned a shoulder and clucked her thick tongue. "Wait, on second thought, crossdressers are the winners."

Stone and the scientists reached an agreement that the winners would share the pleasures of the robot, and the losers would crossdress in the casino. The scientists insisted that the hemlock must demonstrate an audible sound of pleasure, emotion, or evidence of consciousness.

Blue Ishi pushed his arm higher into the hemlock; he pressed his chest to the tree, and reached around the rough slender trunk with his other hand. The blues were perched on the highest branches. The puppets chattered beside the mute child. The scientists, heirs, the wounded, and others waited in a wide circle. Memphis purred and brushed the bark.

Stone and the tribal healers heard trees in their dreams, and the mute child held the hemlock in creation, but no one was sure that the evergreen would respond to convince the scientists, and win the contest with cold reason. The nation waited to hear the stories in the hemlock; to hear a laugh, a moan, to see a wave.

First the crown of the hemlock, and then row after row of needles, turned blue. The scientists strained to see, but heard nothing. The blues laughed and the brown branches turned blue with their humor. The hemlock leaned to the south, and then the blues pointed in the same direction; a floatplane circled the statue and then landed near the Miigis Marina.

"Who is it this time?" shouted Truman.

"Tulip Browne, the investigator," said Stone.

"Who does she want?" asked Gracioso.

"No one, ever," said Stone.

"She heard about the marvelous manicures," said the first lady, but no one listened to him outside the casino. The heirs and healers were bothered by the interruption, because they were certain the

151

hemlock was about to respond to the mute child. The scientists heard nothing, and they were not convinced that the evergreen had pointed to the marina.

The blues teased the branches and the crown of the hemlock burst into a blue radiance once more; the bark was warm, and at last the tree was bright blue. When the mute child withdrew his arm the tree made a human sound; the wounded children heard a moan, two or three words.

"Not that old talking tree trick," said Lappet Tulip Browne. She had arrived with a backpack, and a miniature tape player with classical music. She was not incredulous over the rights and stories of animals and trees, but she was astonished that the obvious was doubtable.

There were thousands of wounded children around in the hemlock; their hands were manicured. The children wore blue puckered moccasins, some with beaded decorations, and most of them wore brown shrouds tied at the waist. At a distance the children could have been a pageant of mutant monks, some with masks.

"Nothing is obvious to science," said Stone.

"Surely, the blue is obvious," said the investigator.

"Color is a light wave, not a truth," said Cantrip.

"Sir, a blue tree is an instance of creation," said Lappet.

"So must a brown tree be," said Cantrip.

"Blue is imagination, not a measure," said Lappet.

"Listen," shouted Truman.

"Our stories in the hemlock," said the panther. The children and the heirs were elated that the robot would be theirs, and the scientists would crossdress that night in the casino. Several scientists were not convinced, a sentient tree was beneath their reason; they pressed their ears to the rough blue bark to listen. The hemlock remembered the blues and the ancient tribes on the point, and whispered a recipe for coarse sweet bread made from her inner bark. The scientists conceded, and the biorobot was marched to the casino for service in the Parthenos Manicure Salon.

Lappet Tulip Browne, the granddaughter of Novena Mae Iron-moccasin and the Baron of Patronia, that wild founder of panic parks and the primal shout, was obsessed with windmills and natural power. The children of the baronage on the reservation were never without obsessions, the tropes to opposition and trickster stories in the blood, and they were healers, each in their own way; healers, never stealers of their inheritance or tribal culture.

She had been hired by the tribal government to investigate the heirs, their politics, their ambitions, and the treatment of tribal children. Wild political notions and malicious disinformation sur-rounded the heirs; one tribal leader was convinced that the cross-bloods had negotiated with foreign criminals to establish a nation of refugees with tribal identities. Welfare agencies had received unfounded reports that some wounded children were being used in biological experiments, and others were abused in porno-graphic films made at Point Assinika.

Lappet was brilliant, stern, and terse; an overbearance, she once told the heirs, that screened invitations to dominance and the colonial gaze; even so she was more at ease with the heirs at the point that she had been on the reservation, or in court. Still, she seemed to be more comfortable with the biorobot than the scien-tists or the crossdressers. She studied men, and now robots, and listened to women, the real world in her creation.

Panda, the biorobot, carried several microcomputers that were told to be sensitive to touch, sound, diction, and oral directions; the bionic memories and mechanical bearings were covered with pliable biochemical synthetic skin. She had the mind of a man, the heart of a robot, and the hands of a woman.

"That thing is creepy, like a guard in reflector sunglasses, you can't ever tell if he's listening, or if he's thinking dirty thoughts," said Harmonia.

"We come together now," said Panda.

"See what I mean?"

"Robots have no natural pose, no manners over their code, no male gaze, we hear the words, but the gestures are synchronized, so the words are clear monotones with no human deceptions," said Lappet.

"You can say that again," said Teets.

"My voice comes from the television," said Panda.

"He's ours, right?" asked Harmonia.

"Yes, our overnight movie," said Teets.

"My voice is overnight," said Panda.

"So, let's make him a woman in the salon," said Harmonia.

"No sex, no genes, no trouble," said Teets.

"Gender is in the computer, not the clothes," said Lappet.

"What could he remember?" asked Harmonia.

"Whatever he hears," she said. Lappet listened to the women and then turned to hear the wind; she could not endure humans without the natural power she heard in the wind, the ocean wind, the cold blue wind from the mountains.

Panda, the first tribal robot, followed the manicurists and investigator to the casino. The mongrels were curious, but held their escape distance under the bingo tables. The biothermionic scent of the robot was monstrous; too clean, no trace of urine, or sweat, no viscous traces in a warm crotch to nose out in memories. The robot turned and shouted "dogs out, dogs out" at the mongrels; the humans were shied, so the mongrels barked back.

Panda had been coded to respond to bingo, the fiscal source of his computer conception; he was so eager to win that he shouted bingo too soon, and the mongrels howled wingo seven times. "Panda wait on wingo," the announcer said with each number, and the robot obeyed.

Lappet was invited to have her nails done; the robot answered the same summons and followed in slow motion through the double doors and sat down beside her in the Parthenos Manicure Salon.

"Creepy, he's got cold horny nails," said Harmonia.

"Panda be mine," said Teets.

"He could probably be a nice person, but I never did get along with electronic things, like cash registers and computers, they want too much from me," said Harmonia.

Panda hummed with contentment, a low robotic tone, acoustic noise, as the manicurists told stories, and then listened to the investigator. Lappet told them about the miniature windmills in her condominium, how the ocean wind "turns the copper blades, faster and faster, a paradise of purrs in the rush of a storm."

"So, what's up with the investigation?" asked Teets.

"The subtle reproach," said Lappet.

"Not really, but we wonder why anyone would be an investigator for a corrupt tribal government, and always believe the things that evil people say," said Teets.

"That's not the issue," said Lappet.

"Why not?" asked Harmonia.

"The tribe has received complaints that child welfare laws have been violated, and paid me to investigate and report my observations to them," said Lappet.

"Since when do they care about children?" asked Harmonia.

"Stone heals these children, no one else ever cares about them, and that bothers those big bellies on the reservation more than anything, they don't trust people who do good things," said Teets. She defended the nation, the heirs, the children, and indicted the enemies of trickster stories, humor, and healers, she impeached those who fear the liberation of the mind.

Lappet told the manicurists that the tribal government and various federal agencies were convinced that the heirs were selling tribal enrollment documents to refugees who could then enter the country and claim services as a tribal person; this would reduce services on reservations.

"Who could believe that?" said Harmonia.

"No one but elected politicians," said Teets.

"However, in this instance the tribal government resisted the rumors, but federal agents insisted that the tribe report on the refugees and on the alleged sexual abuses of children, not by the heirs, of course, but by one or more of the scientists," said Lappet.

Teets was disheartened by the suspicion of sexual abuse by the scientists; she understood from personal experiences the horrors of survival in some tribal families, but who could be so cruel to abuse wounded children, those burned by the poisons and chemical pleasures of civilization; abused even more by the men who were trusted to heal them. She cried over the memories of the cruelties the children had endured.

Lappet reported to the tribal government that she would continue her investigation of one scientist, but otherwise there was no evidence of child abuse, and the rumors of refugees at the new nation were unfounded. She pointed out, however, that the heirs considered the idea a proper response to the corruption in tribal leadership on reservations, and would soon provide artists and the wounded refugees of the world with tribal identities at Point Assinika.

"Stone Columbus, as you know, is the son of Binn Columbus, and that white man who refused to disclose his name; genealogical records confirm beyond a doubt that he is a crossblood, although he has never been enrolled as a legal member of the tribe, because his grandparents Truman Columbus, an assumed surname, were opposed to the political reductions of identities," the investigator reported to the tribal president.

Lappet continued in her report with a revelation about the first lady that would confound his son and the heirs. "University records reveal that a man with his exact description was a woman; a professor of consciousness named Michele Lavant. However, he was retired with a cash settlement when affirmative action investigators discovered that she was in fact a man named Michel Lavant. He dressed as a woman to land a teaching position at a time when white men were seldom considered. No one noticed the unvoiced letter at the end of his given name; that single letter was the cue to his gender and politics. He had earned his doctorate under the name Michel, but university officials either ignored, or took no notice of Michele, the name he entered on his applications.

"The names were viewed by lawyers as subtle misrepresentation, but not fraud; one professor described the situation as a "crossname simulation on a bait and switch affirmative action application." Michel earned some praise and humor when he bared his chest.

Radical feminists had been haunted by her masculine manners and tragic metaphors; their challenge, for ideological reasons, of her courageous code and true gender, instigated the investigation that resulted in his golden parachute from the university. That he was an outstanding teacher did not seem to matter in the rush to gender reparations.

Tribal police records confirm that a man with no name, a weaver, had been seen on the reservation within months of his separation from the university. Peculiar poses, indeed, but his behavior was rational. "There is nothing in his background to suggest that he would abuse children; rather, he has demonstrated natural affection."

Lappet reported that it was impossible to assess negative or positive public responses to the crossblood heirs and their enterprises. "Stone has earned wide public admiration, and romantic love for his imagination and dedication to heal tribal children. There is no clear evidence that he has been influenced, as the tribal police suspected, by the eighteenth century lawyer of the Cherokee Nation, Sir Alexander Cumming.

"Stone has indicated on talk radio, however, that he would, if he could, create a sovereign nation for Sephardic Jews, but he has no obvious plans to do so at Point Assinika. Louis Riel, it would appear, has influenced him more than Cumming."

Lappet concluded her report with praise for the heirs and the ideals of the new nation; such personal conclusions were unprecedented in her ten years as an investigator. "You would be more responsible to tribal people if you supported the humor and courage of this nation, rather than tolerating disinformation about the Heirs of Christopher Columbus." She was never paid for her services.

Lappet maintained her condominium, but that spring she moved to the new nation. She established a legal services center with worldwide representation, and provided legal advice on genetic implant research, the development of biorobotics, and universal tribal identities, sustained by bingo and international court decisions, for tribal children, refugees, and Sephardic Jews.

"One day this nation may provide more reliable bionic leaders on the reservations than the natural ration of male genes has produced in the past several hundred thousand years," she told a *New York Times* reporter at a press conference on biorobotics.

Panda and three new biorobots were trained to heal with humor; their memories held the best trickster stories, and modern variations, that would liberate the mind and heal the bodies of children. Overnight, Uta Moot was named the foremost robotics engineer in the world; she lived with Panda and Blue Ishi on Miigis Marina.

The wounded children trusted their robots at first sight in the casino; the new children, lonesome and abused, told the robots their secrets, more than they ever told the manicurists. Moot trained the robots to be tender, responsive, and they remembered the children in their stories; the robots were not capable of emotional double binds, dead letter promises, or induced dependencies. Nurturance comes at a heinous cost in a consumer culture.

Lappet persuaded the engineers to design a miniature windmill that would generate enough power to run the salon, the casino, laboratories, the marina, and the lights on the Trickster of Liberty.

The windmills purred, a natural power on the point. The push of the wind over the wide blades was heard at night on the Strait of Georgia. She mounted hundreds of blue windmills on the pavilions, on the borders, and the Miigis Marina.

BLOOD TITHES

Louis Riel wore a black coat and blue moccasins that late autumn of his death. "I thank God for having given me the strength to die well," he said to the priest on the stairs to the cold, cold gallows platform. "I am on the threshold of eternity and I do not want to turn back. . . . I thank all those who helped me in my misfortunes." His hands were bound, and then the silent executioner covered his head with a cotton hood.

Riel, inspiration of the métis resistance, was convicted of high treason and sentenced to death. He wrote to government leaders during the few months he waited to be hanged; he was seditious to the end for the rights and claims of tribal members and the métis in Canada.

"I have only this," he said, and touched his heart when the sheriff asked if he had any last wishes to dispose of his meager properties. "I was willing to give it to my country fifteen years ago, and it is all I have to give now. . . . You will see that I had a mission to perform."

Riel "quivered and swayed on the taut rope," wrote Joseph Kinsey Howard in *Strange Empire*. "The official witnesses, white-faced and sick, watched the body jerk on the rope, watched it sway in a narrowing arc like a medicine bundle dangling from the pole of the sun dance lodge."

159

Stone was heartened by the wild heat of his resistance and spiritual visions, but not by the cold weather of his tragic creeds. The heirs pursued the same mission of resistance and tribal independence, but theirs liberated the mind with the pleasures of trickster humor, and held no prisoners in the heart.

Hartwell Bowsfield wrote in *Louis Riel: The Rebel and the Hero* that he mailed a letter to "United States President Grover Cleveland, outlining the wrongs he said had been committed by the Canadian government against the people of the Northwest and suggesting that the United States annex the country."

Stone wrote to the president several generations later, in the name and memories of the métis resistance, and demanded the tithe due the Heirs of Christopher Columbus. "My lawyers have advised me that according to precedent in international courts we are due, as documented heirs, the tithe of our namesake, for the past five centuries.

"King Ferdinand and Queen Isabella signed seven documents and granted to 'Don Cristóbal de Colón in some satisfaction for what he hath discovered in the ocean sea,' a tenth of the gold, and other precious metals, spices, pearls, gems, and other merchandise obtained in commerce and free of all taxes.

"These rights and capitulations have never been abrogated by treaties, conquest, or purchase; therefore, since we are the legal heirs of the unpaid tithe on this continent, be so advised, that unless your government pays the inheritance due, we shall annex, as satisfaction of the tithe, the United States of America."

Chaine Riel Doumet was the best investigator the tribe could hire to report on the stone tavern and the megabingo barge; he was related to the métis leader through his mother, and he was a retired military intelligence agent. He testified at the hearing in federal court and has continued his investigation for the tribe; later, when satellite surveillance revealed a hot spot at Point Assinika, he was called back to service. His natural cover, if he needed one as an intelligence operative, was that of a private investigator for the tribal government.

Chaine used a portable word processor and modem. To separate his documents he reported with his first name to the tribal president and with his second name to military intelligence. The reports to the tribe were couched in binaries and metaphors that resolved rumors and suspicions; on the other hand, the modem transmissions to central intelligence were scenarios and probabilities. He was a crossblood natural at the remains of chance in oral tribal stories, but less practiced at the simulations of political evidence and consumer notices. At the same time he made observations in a personal third narrative.

Chaine reported, with a casual prologue in both modem reports, that "civilization and panic holes created on a natural meadow at the headwaters, and the stone tavern were chartered by the Heirs of Christopher Columbus in the autumn of 1868, the same year the White Earth Reservation was established in northern Minnesota. Susan B. Anthony founded a suffragette newspaper, *The Revolution*, in that year, and the Fourteenth Amendment to the Constitution was adopted." He was pleased to note that the "McIlhenny Tabasco Company was established at Avery Island, Louisiana, at the same time. This year, some five generations later, the first tribal nation has been declared at Point Assinika."

Riel reported, "Stone told the world on talk radio that his scientists had isolated the ultimate tribal power of his ancestors, the healer genes. At first no one paid much attention to the crossblood who made a fortune at bingo, tribal leaders were serious about the money, not the dreamers, but then there were reliable reports that tribal children with birth defects and other mutants were being healed with sacred tribal genes."

Chaine told the tribal president that "Stone was no longer a problem on the reservation since he created a new nation on October 12, 1992, at Point Assinika. However, he has initiated, with the capable advice of his lawyer, Lappet Browne, tribal enrollment records for crossblood artists and others. There is no evidence that this would be a problem to reservations, unless, of course, the tribes resist these new identities in tribal, state, and federal courts."

Riel reported that "Indian artists, according to recent federal laws, as you know, must be members of a tribe, or certified by a tribal government. The purpose of the law is to protect the representation of tribal artists, but no one considered how many artists were not tribal members. Indians who were authentic under the new law, certified with tribal identity cards, had a distinct advantage in the art market.

"Stone bucked the political dominance of tribal leaders and created identity cards for tribal artists that were based on the recognition of peers, rather than the choice of tribal politicians," reported Riel.

"Stone resists the notion of blood quantums, racial identification, and tribal enrollment. The heir is a crossblood, to be sure, but there is more to his position than mere envy of unbroken tribal blood. Indians, he said, are 'forever divided by the racist arithmetic measures of tribal blood.' He would accept anyone who wanted to be tribal, 'no blood attached or scratched,' he once said on talk radio.

"He points out how many people have faked their tribal blood, 'so if it's so easy to fake blood then why bother with the measures?' His point is to make the world tribal, a universal identity, and return to other values as measures of human worth, such as the dedication to heal rather than steal tribal cultures.

"However, his most disputable promise is a genetic implant that could be used to prove not only paternity, but national and racial identities, and forensic genetics. Their scientists have established the genetic signatures of most of the tribes in the country, so that anyone could, with an injection of suitable genetic material, prove beyond a doubt a genetic tribal identity. Germans, at last, could be genetic Sioux, and thousands of coastal blondes bored with being white could become shadow tribes of Hopi, or Chippewa, with gene therapies from Point Assinika," reported Riel.

Chaine reported to the tribal president that he should be concerned, but the notion of a universal tribe would cause no harm, "because there was nothing to lose but racial distance."

Riel reported to central intelligence that "tribal governments should consider the scenarios of identity because the measures of blood quantums have reduced the tribes to racist colonies. Meanwhile, federal agencies could be burdened with increased claims for services; the worst scenario would be the legal and political demands for new reservations, and even massive increases in refugee populations on existing reservations.

"University students might choose to become tribal and declare the campus a new reservation, or suppose, in another scenario, that the number of new 'Stone Age Indians,' as tribal leaders speak of them, became ten million, including refugees, at the White Earth Reservation," he continued. "Indeed, the heirs are cross-blood tricksters with their own scenarios."

Riel told central that it would be "wise to assume that tribal artists would celebrate the virtues of their new tribal identities with a new nation; moreover, there would, no doubt, be eager constituencies at universities."

Chaine reported to the tribal president that the "tithe claimed by the heirs would cause no problems on the reservation." However, he told the agencies that the "heirs would stimulate popular support with their appeal to the International Court of Justice at the Hague."

The Heirs of Christopher Columbus were determined to negotiate a cash settlement or some other agreement to resolve the tithe due for the past five centuries. Lappet Browne reasoned that once the tithe was being considered as a dispute between states by the International Court of Justice, the United States and Canada would never overturn Point Assinika.

Riel reported to the agencies that the "potential for public adversities is not tribal, but remains with the federal government; no matter what the proposed resolution, the public would support the heirs, the new nation, and that because of talk radio since the earlier success of the bingo barge on Lake of the Woods. However, it would be unwise to understate the dedication of the heirs to heal children and better the world with humor."

"These realities," he reported to both the tribal president and the agencies, "make it all the more difficult for me to report that my most recent investigation has revealed the sexual abuse of children by a genetic scientist at Point Assinika. If the abuse and pornographic materials were not enough to bear, the scientist is believed to be an escaped death camp medical doctor responsible for cruel biological experiments and the extermination of thousands of Jews at Auschwitz.

"Pir Cantrip is an escaped Nazi, according to the records in various military archives. I have not witnessed the abuse, and he does not appear in the photographs with nude disabled children. My information, in part, comes from confidential sources, and from intelligence reports on doctors at the concentration camps.

"There is no evidence that any other scientists are involved, or that the heirs even know about the abuse or photographs. The Nazi doctor established the research laboratories and was able to isolate the genetic code carried by the heirs; he proved their inheritance. Cantrip has avoided public attention. His reputation as the doctor who saves deformed children would be difficult to rebuke, even with an indictment for sex crimes. The man is loved, rather vulnerable, but he is ruled by his weakness."

Riel reported that the "scientists are only part of the healing, as you know. The heirs, and a collection of people too incredible to describe, for instance, a former priest turned manicurist, are the paramount healers. They do this with stories and humor, and what they say becomes, in some way, the energy that heals. This story energy somehow influences the genetic codes and the children are mended in one way or another.

"I was fortunate to observe a deformed tribal child in the process of being healed," reported Riel. "She was transformed in such a way that was hard for me to believe. The child was born with no hands, a crooked spine, a malformed chin that protruded to the side, and exposed uneven teeth.

"Doctor Cantrip x-rayed and photographed the child, and prepared her for a genetic implant. It was impossible then to think about his perversion, and the abuse of children. Later she was taken to a comfortable room with subdued lights. The heirs and, much to my surprise, the robots told her stories. Several small blue women touched her, and the rest was truly a miracle. The child was amused by the stories, but she seemed only half awake as her body strained to become whole.

"I was astounded by the power of the genes from the heirs, and the changes in her body," he reported to the agencies. "First, two miniature hands appeared on her arms. The stumps sprouted, and the hands grew out of the thick skin just the right size for her body, as if the genes also carried the memories of her age. Then her spine and chin were touched by the blue women, and her face and teeth moved into line. These were the powers of the shamans our elders remembered from the tribal past."

Chaine reported later to the tribal president that "Doric Michéd caused the death of Felipa Flowers at St. George's Parish in Gravesend, England. He was determined to recover the remains of Christopher Columbus, so he assaulted and tied her down in an abandoned building. Doric will not be charged because the cause of death cannot be determined; furthermore, he denies the assault and stated that he saw her on the street near the church, nothing more. The investigation has continued because of an insistent rare book dealer and a police captain from New York."

Riel told the agencies that "Pellegrine Treves, a book collector from London, and Captain Treves Brink, who bear the same name from distant relatives, have been persistent investigators into the death of Felipa Flowers. Their constant attention has become one more unusual scenario in this case, the twists and turns of national and religious identities.

"Sephardic Jews have been in their stories of inheritance from the first days at the stone tavern, and it is no accident that the burial ground of the heirs is named the House of Life," reported Riel. "There is no question that the heirs have pursued their mythic connections to the lost tribes. Here, the heirs have imagined their union with Mayan hand talkers and the stories in the Bible of the ten lost tribes of Israel.

"The significance of their inheritance could be measured by certain historical probabilities and the inheritance of their genetic code. The denial of their unusual origins would be a cold shoulder to the sacred stories, true or not, that the heirs have woven with the politics of genes and bingo. Stone would say that to best the trickster stories is to overturn civilization with humor. The agencies would be imprudent to understate the significance of these stories and historical connections, however imaginative."

Riel continued, "Whether the heirs believe their stories is not the point, because no culture would last long under the believer test; the point is that humor has political significance and as a scenario, no government has ever been praised for the reduction of communal humor.

"Stone has said that 'this is a marvelous world of tricksters, no panic holes are deep enough to hold my rage,' an idea he borrowed from the crossblood Griever de Hocus. The best scenarios here are for the government to listen more to talk radio and encourage the wounded and deformed to travel in large numbers to Point Assinika."

Riel concluded with a personal report to the agencies on the wicked activities of operatives. "I am shamed to learn that the tavern stone was stolen at the headwaters by federal agents. The heirs would say, if they knew, that the operatives deserve the horrors of their crime. In this case, however, the scientists commissioned to study the energy and powers of the stone for military purposes have suffered the most. They lost their vision, and diseases resulting from bioelectrical aberrations have afflicted those who touched the stone.

"I cannot believe that our agents dumped the stone in the ocean. This information cannot be kept from the heirs, the tribal government, or the public forever. The erosion of public credibility would be serious. The only possible scenarios would be complete disclosure, a short-term crisis; any massive disinformation campaign would further discredit the agencies, not the heirs, in the long run."

Chaine reported to the tribal president that for "reasons of cultural identity he was obliged to breach security over a most ominous condition that could menace the tribe and cause enormous harm to the nation and the Heirs of Christopher Columbus.

"I have shared this same information with the heirs. Please consider and understand that any public disclosure would be denied by me and the agencies, and you can be sure that you would never hear from me again.

"Military operatives learned from their bingo informants that the wiindigoo was frozen in a cave, the natural state of the ice woman who held the tribal world in balance. With no central authorization the wiindigoo was stolen by racist field agents and thawed out. Clearly this was an act of subversive vengeance for the harm caused by the tavern stone the same agents had stolen from the headwaters.

"I was called back from early retirement, as you know, after twenty years in covert military operations, only to be discouraged by the savages of intelligence. I regret that my career has ended with such disheartening information."

MOCCASIN GAME

The Trickster of Liberty was obscured in a close fog once more at the point. The rough boards on the marina were mellow in the morning, fast and loose conversations carried from the casino, horns sounded hard by the sea, and creation stories were overheard in the wild blood.

Stone posed at the end of the marina, adrift in memories; he ruled the wash of waves, but he could not see the water. The stones from the meadow were closer in his vision than the statue and pavilions. The blue puppets chattered in the hemlock.

Miigis and Blue Ishi hummed and soughed as they stepped on every other board to the end of the marina. Admire was at their side, cautious in the dense fog; she listened, the sounds were richer than scent.

Pellegrine Treves wrote that he would arrive on the morning ferry; one by one the heirs gathered at the marina to meet the rare book collector and hear his stories. His letter was brief, no one knew what he had learned about the murder of Felipa Flowers.

The sun and a light breeze raised the fog late in the morning, and the heirs watched the statue emerge with a blue radiance; Pellegrine chartered a floatplane because the ferry was delayed by the weather; the plane circled the statue and landed on the calm bay.

"Mister Columbus," said Treves.

"Call me Stone."

"Stone, of course, are these your children then?" asked Treves. He waited on the marina for directions; the heirs smiled and watched him, but no one answered. His arrival seemed inconvenient, so he became more formal. "Pellegrine Treves is my name, from London."

"My name is Teets."

"Harmonia Dewikwe, and we're from the salon."

"Indeed, so pleased to meet you, and the weather has cleared nicely, but still a bit cold from the fog," said Treves. His manner was precious, as he was distracted by the blue child.

The pilot of the floatplane unloaded two suitcases, one aluminum and sealed with tape. Miigis, the luminous child, and Blue Ishi carried the metallic brown suitcase, the remains of Pocahontas.

"Listen, the heirs have been rather silent about things," said Luckie White. "Nothing personal, its the anticipation of what you have to tell about the murder."

"Certainly," said Treves.

"Have you heard my talk radio show?"

"Sorry, afraid not," said Treves.

"Luckie White, the admiral of Carp Radio," she said. "You might say without exaggeration that this nation owes its public support to talk radio, the truth in the wild night."

"Quite, and a national experience," said Treves.

"Stone is a healer in his stories, and he discovered the course of humor that heals here, but others are determined to hold him to the discoveries of a place, an image, a nation," said Luckie.

"Truly, as if objects could be discovered alone," said Treves.

"Yes, yes, objects can be lost once we have them, but how can a place be an object, or be discovered like a continent, when no one knew what it would become?" said Luckie. "I mean, how could Columbus know he had discovered America, or that his heirs would be healers?"

"I should think language is our trick of discovery, what we name is certain to become that name, but tell me, are these the subjects that you discussed on your radio program?" asked Treves.

169

"The truth in the dark," said Luckie.

"I should think you would feel a great satisfaction," said Treves.

"Stone is the dreamer, and he was a great talker on radio, he loved it, and even carried his own microphone around for a time, but since the death of Felipa he's been closer to silence, or as he says, closer to the stone," she said and paused at the base of the Trickster of Liberty.

"I understand," said Treves.

"Stone commissioned the Trickster of Liberty and it was ready when we landed and declared this place the sovereign nation of Point Assinika," said Luckie.

"What does that mean?" asked Treves.

"Assinika means stones, the place of the stones," she said, and seemed to wonder. Luckie pointed out the blue medicine poles, the spirit catchers, the bear paw on the flag, the pavilions, laboratories, the blues that heal, and at last the Parthenos Manicure Salon.

"Forgive me, the children draw one's attention," said Treves.

"They come by the thousands to be healed, abandoned children, the tribal mutants who bear the curse of a chemical civilization," said Luckie.

"Stone created the nation for children, then?" he asked. Treves was brushed and touched by wounded children, some with radiant hands, and others wore blue moccasins.

"Stone once said he has done nothing to be bored, that and humor has been his only mission in the world, and the rest of the time he says he dreams out of time," said Luckie.

"You seem to know him so well," said Treves.

"Somehow people show themselves more on talk radio, more than they might even to their own families, and he told me about everything," said Luckie.

"Talk radio must be a clever resistance," said Treves.

"The children with blue moccasins have been healed, they bear the genetic signature of survivance from ancient Mayan hand talkers, and the genes inherited from Christopher Columbus," she said. Luckie was pleased to tell the stories of the heirs and the nation. She once raised the very same questions that she now answers; a talk radio condition, she warned the producers, that comes too close to trickster stories, "your questions are my very answers."

Pellegrine toured the casino, praised the first lady, and then he was convinced that a manicure would "absolve his worries in the New World." He hesitated at first, of course, but he was bound by manners and courtesy not to resist the peculiar invitation.

Teets held his left hand, and Harmonia was at his right side; each would have a hand to manicure. In minutes he was at ease and content, as they had promised, despite the heirs and others who crowded around his chair in the salon. He understood that this was the time he should tell them about Pocahontas and Felipa Flowers.

Stone, his daughter Miigis, and Blue Ishi with Panda the robot waited at the side of the chair. The heirs and others behind the manicure chair were Luckie White, the talk radio admiral; Truman the shouter and the croaker; Binn, who heard containers; Memphis, the black panther; Samana, the shaman bear and hand talker; Gracioso, the panic hole historian; Caliban, the great white mongrel; Almost, the laser healer; Lappet, the lawyer and windmill designer; Admire, the healer with the blue tongue; Uta Moot, the creator of robots; Teets, Harmonia, and Padrino de Torres, the manicurists; Eleanor Roosevelt, and the other crossdressers.

"Do you like my ears?" asked Teets.

"Yes, lovely," said Treves.

"Stone healed my ears and straightened my smile, so what do you think about my face?" she asked, and smiled to show her bright even teeth.

"Truly wonderful," said Treves.

"Do you like my head?" asked Harmonia.

"Healed as well?"

"No, you see this is the third one, and it saved my life, so, for now, this is me, what you see, no more other heads on the horizon," she said. Harmonia turned her head from side to side so he could see.

"Quite marvelous," said Treves.

"Felipa and Columbus are buried here, you know, we moved them from the meadow near the headwaters," said Binn. She

171

brushed the bits of fingernail and cuticle into a container and placed it with thousands of others on the shelves. He was listening to the first lady and did not notice the outlandish practice.

"Doric murdered her, didn't he," shouted Truman.

"Yes, with poison," said Treves.

"Tell us the whole thing," said Gracioso.

"Everything," purred Memphis.

"Doric Michéd told me he was a man named Transom, a shaman, and he persuaded me to contact Felipa," said Treves. "As you know, she agreed to come to London to receive the remains of Pocahontas."

"Transom is dead too," said Caliban.

"His body has never been found," said the radiant shaman with her hands. Samana was behind the chair; the image he saw in the mirror was the image of a bear. He closed his eyes several times to confirm that he saw a bear, and then he turned to see her face and the bear vanished.

"Doric, we learned, had Felipa followed after lunch from the explorers club, which explains how he was able to locate Transom later, so he did, of course, and we presume his body will be found one day," said Treves.

"Transom was a mongrel shaman," said Caliban.

"I really wouldn't know," said Treves.

"Transom was a crossdresser," said the first lady.

"Indeed he was," said Treves.

"So, what happened next?" asked Harmonia.

"Happen next, next," repeated Panda.

"Never mind what happens now," said Padrino.

"Happen now, now," repeated Panda.

"Well, Doric Michéd dressed as he thought Transom would, befriended me in London for the sole purpose of kidnapping Felipa, in the vain hope that he could trade the remains of Pocahontas for those of Columbus," said Treves.

"How would you know?" asked Harmonia.

"Exactly, I had no reason to be suspicious, however, when I met

Doric later he was the same person, but with a nasty scar on his cheek," said Treves.

"So, how did you find out that he killed Felipa?" asked Luckie. She reached toward him, as if she held a microphone, a habit from talk radio she could not break.

"The moccasins, the pine, and the scar, of course," said Treves.

"What happened to her moccasins?" asked Stone.

"Yes, the moccasins were missing when her body was found at the base of the statue, and she told me about carrying a sprig of white pine, and that was missing too," said Treves. "Later, we found them in a car hired by one Doric Michéd."

Treves withdrew his hands from the manicurists and opened his leather briefcase. Inside were the blue moccasins that Felipa wore at the time of her death; he handed them to the luminous child.

"We dream the mistle thrush," said Miigis.

"Felipa wore this one out," said Stone. He laughed over a tiny hole on the sole of the right moccasin. "She wore them for good luck, and her luck wore out in London."

"Doric knew as much, that's why he removed them when he killed her, and stole the sprig of white pine that she carried for protection," said Treves.

"Bald eagles wear pine," said Panda.

"No, no, eagles nest with white pine," said the first lady.

"Yes, white pine nests," said Panda.

"I've been all over the world as a book collector, but this is the first time a robot ever talked to me, and it seems to make sense," said Treves.

"Listen, talking is one thing, listening is another," croaked Truman. "Panda remembers, that's what robots are supposed to do, but can he outwit his creator?"

"Never outwit creators," said Panda.

"So, back to the story, how did you find out who murdered Felipa?" asked Luckie. She was impatient for conclusions, a worldview that was frustrated by the heirs who imagine the starts but never the ends.

Pellegrine Treves returned to the manicure chair and continued his stories. Teets polished the nails on his left hand; Harmonia painted his nails on the other hand. He watched the heirs and the bear in the mirror on the wall in front of the chair.

Felipa bashed Doric on the cheek with the metal case, he told them, and the wound left a noticeable scar. She was shrouded and carried to a room in an abandoned building across the street from St. George's Parish.

"Captain Treves Brink, a very distant relative, of course, saved the day in the investigation," said Treves. "He knew how to get to the hidden facts and did so with what appeared to be little effort."

"But how did he get involved?" asked Gracioso.

"Captain Brink and Felipa were friends, I gathered, and he spoke of a hearing in your federal courts, but in any case, he uncovered the scheme that may have caused her death," said Treves.

"Christopher Columbus?" asked Luckie.

"Who else?" said Caliban.

"The remains, you see, had been promised by the president of the explorers club, with a price reported to be at least ten million dollars, for reburial in a quincentenary mausoleum dedicated to Christopher Columbus in the Dominican Republic," said Treves.

"Doric was suckered by the museum?" croaked Truman.

"Indeed, duped by the Brotherhood of American Explorers, and his need to appear important drove him to compete for a better price, for some personal gain, or perhaps he thought he could sell a small portion of the remains to the Heirs of Columbus," said Treves.

"That's all the heirs needed for their scientists to document the genetic signature of survivance, just a bit of bone, or even a touch of dried blood from the ball that was found at the bottom of the casket," said Luckie.

Pellegrine Treves continued the stories in the salon. His hands were radiant. Doric had obtained a lethal venom from equatorial traders, who were in fact intelligence agents, according to an informal investigation by Captain Brink. The venom, however, does not leave a trace in the body, and there was no evidence that such a tribal venom caused the death of Felipa Flowers.

"Captain Brink deserves the honors for the rescue of the remains of Pocahontas and the arrest of Doric," said Treves. "Together, we baited Doric to sell the remains for two million dollars, a price he could not resist, and he agreed to deliver the metal case to New York.

"Naturally, we were waiting for him at the airport, and he was arrested on various charges from grave robbery to the possession of stolen historical relics," said Treves.

"So, where are the remains?" asked Luckie.

"Pocahontas is here, I can tell you that much, and Doric faces a trial on felony charges, but no more than that," he said. Treves was sworn not to reveal that the remains had been substituted. The metal case held for trial evidence contained anonymous remains. Doric had no way to prove the identity of the remains, and the prosecution would not depend on specific remains.

Doric was convicted on one felony charge and released on parole; there was never more than circumstantial evidence to charge him with the murder of Felipa Flowers in England.

Binn Columbus, however, heard the stories of her death in the blue moccasins. Binn held the moccasins to her ear and said that two men tied her down in a room, one man touched her breasts, the other man with the blood on his cheek watched and then he injected a poison into her thigh. Felipa dreamed that she was a mistle thrush in the tree over the church, she flew into a wicked storm and never returned.

The salon was silent. Teets and Harmonia wiped the tears from their eyes. Admire licked the heirs with her blue tongue. Panda tried to whistle a tune from the *New World* Symphony, but her mouth was not designed for music.

Pellegrine told the heirs that federal agents had initiated vicious but believable disinformation about them and the scientific research at Point Assinika. Pir Cantrip, for instance, had been named as a war criminal and a sex pervert, when in fact he had survived the death camps. Treves said that "false records were created and made available to at least one investigator."

"Yes, but we never believe anything the government has ever said about the tribes, least of all the information about the heirs and our nation," said Stone.

"Major Chaine Doumet was given false information about Cantrip, who is an honorable Sephardic Jew, and about your demands for money from the United States," said Treves.

"Pir Cantrip heals children, he loves their humor, and he is a wounded Jew, but Chaine was right about the blood tithe due the heirs of the great explorer," said Lappet. "Either the government pays the tithe or we plan to annex the nation."

"Seriously, how could you do that?" asked Treves.

"Trickster healers, bingo, and talk radio for a start," said Stone.

"The opposition would be too much," said Treves.

"We heal with opposition, we are held together with opposition, not separation, or silence, and the best humor in the world is pinched from opposition," he said. Stone moved closer to the mirror, so close that his hot breath misted the reflection of his smile.

The Heirs of Columbus held reburial ceremonies for Felipa Flowers, Pocahontas, and Christopher Columbus; their remains were sealed in vaults at the House of Life near the base of the Trickster of Liberty.

Caliban wore a brown wool dress, orange stockings, and carried a purple shoulder bag that night. Lady Bird Johnson was in a black suit with an enormous artificial wildflower. The heirs and the healed children wore blue moccasins. Uta Moot dressed the robots in lingerie, one red and one white; Panda wore blue and tried once more to whistle a tune.

Stone wore his red tunic and carried the bear paw banner and teased the blues in the hemlock. He posed on the marina and roared to remember the lightning and thunderstorms. Miigis danced in a blue robe; she was radiant that night and told stories about the world she saw in dreams with birds. Blue Ishi, ever at her side, touched the stones and statue, and the vault turned blue in the House of Life.

Judge Beatrice Lord and Captain Treves Brink arrived by ferry for the ceremonies; they praised the healers and the children, and pledged their support of the sovereignty at Point Assinika.

The judge wore an embroidered mistle thrush on her bertha collar; she brought several containers with her for a listen by Binn Columbus. The music box was overloaded with parlor gossip about children, antique store gossip about prices; the leather backpack held lusty stories by a couple on a mountain; the cigarette lighter revealed only half-finished sentences. Binn agreed to hear the evidence in trial exhibits from time to time for the judge.

The ceremonies continued until the morning star appeared just before sunrise. The mongrels barked at the planet. Admire licked the wounded children who had fallen asleep on the shore near the statue. The miniature windmills purred on the marina, and the bear paw banners brightened the new nation at dawn.

Point Assinika would have been a nation that healed with opposition and humor, and without the worries that wounded children, but on that sublime morning as the star baited the pines in the east and bounced on the bay, the mongrels were silenced, the wind weakened on the windmills, and the blues retreated to the hemlock. The rumors were true that the wiindigoo, the handsome cannibal who devours children, had been thawed out by federal operatives, an act of vengeance because two agents were burned by the stolen tavern stone. The wiindigoo soughed at the morning star and told the heirs that the time had come at last to finish the moccasin game.

Padrino de Torres, unaware of the wiindigoo, persuaded the captain and the judge to sit for a manicure; the judge knew him as a priest and she was surprised that he had turned to hands. She understood the pleasures of a manicure but never considered that children would be honored and healed by the solicitous care of their hands.

Teets and Harmonia manicured the captain, one on each hand. The captain had been cued by the book collector to rave over the beauty of ears, a new smile, and a wooden head. He did so, but on the opposite side; the manicurists mocked him and then demanded an encore.

Binn was there to collect the cuttings and bits of cuticle from the judge and captain. Later she brought their bits together in a tumbler and told the wild sex scenes she heard in the container. Luckie, Lappet, Harmonia, Teets, Uta, and Eleanor Roosevelt, the wise women of the nation, laughed over the ruts and mock wails of judicial orgasms in the Parthenos Manicure Salon.

The wiindigoo, the cannibal who wore a sweet scent to enchant children, never learned the wisdom of the morning star; he was a mutant demon with no vision, no shadow, and no interest in the planets.

Black Elk, the common tribal man with a great vision, said that those who see the "morning star shall see more" and be wise. "Things in the sky shall be like relatives."

John Neihardt created certain poetic tribal visions in his narrative, the "beginning and the ending are mine," in *Black Elk Speaks*. The omission of translated stories told by Black Elk, however, would have more bearing on the destinies of the heirs and the course of events at Point Assinika.

Black Elk learned the power of two herbs in his great visions; the first was the star herb that healed, and the second was the destructive herb of war, the "soldier weed" was the brute force of evil and termination. "This was the most powerful herb of all that I had gotten," said Black Elk. "It could be used in war and could destroy a nation."

Black Elk told Neihardt that the war herb "was too terrible to use," so terrible that the translation of his vision of the herb was deleted from the published narrative *Black Elk Speaks*.

Stone Columbus was given a similar war herb in a dream, a vision of healers, and the herb was so invincible and ruinous to the world, that surveillance satellites revealed a radiant shadow on the point. Several nations hired operatives, who posed as scientists and even the wounded, to locate and describe this potential weapon.

The wiindigoo marched to the end of the marina; his evil manner turned the weather, music lost to hideous moans, breath

178

to hollow bone; children would be devoured, and the heirs would become skeletons if the demon won the moccasin game.

The last game at the headwaters was close to the end of the tribe; the wiindigoo was about to reach for the moccasin with the marked coin, when the ice woman blew on his hands and head and he was frozen solid that summer. He would have won if the ice woman had not come to save the children from the water demons; she held the wiindigoo in ice at the back of her cave on the island in Lake of the Woods.

"His summer would be our end," said the bear shaman with her hands. Samana was a hand talker from the island; she praised the winter as a bear and honored the ice woman. The heirs have done the same since he was frozen, but now the wiindigoo has returned to finish the game.

"He was thawed by the government," said Binn.

"Once more, he should have been fed to the mongrels, piece by evil piece, bone by rotten bone, and scattered in a hundred gopher holes," said Caliban.

Binn Columbus listened to the four blue moccasins, and then she placed them in a precise row near the House of Life and the Trickster of Liberty. One pair were hers, and the other moccasins had been worn by Felipa Flowers.

Truman shouted that blue moccasins were a natural balance, "there is nothing to fear from evil men who wear hard leather." The mongrels nosed the old moccasins with caution.

The wiindigoo waited on the marina until the heirs were prepared to play the game. "Remember, this is your last game, the children are mine, nothing is more real than a moccasin game to the death." The robots turned at his side and repeated, as a human would mock, "the children are mine" and "the dead moccasins, the dead moccasins."

Truman croaked that the heirs would remember this as their best moccasin game. "The game that saved the heirs from the water demons, there is nothing to lose at the feet of the Trickster of Liberty."

Pir Cantrip, Uta Moot, and the other scientists did not understand the histories or the seriousness of the moccasin game with the cannibal; they were told once more, "if the wiindigoo wins the heirs and tribal children would vanish." Pir was convinced that the heirs were somehow in readiness to overturn the demon at his own game.

The Trickster of Liberty was a vital sign in the spotlights. The heirs and others came together on one side of the moccasins with the statue and casino behind them. The night was clear, the stars were bright. The children circled the vaults, curious and overcrowded on all sides of the game.

Stone placed a dose of the war herb in a pouch under the moccasin with the marked coin, the copper coin that bears the image of the great explorer. The war herb was under the last moccasin in the row, the one worn by Felipa Flowers.

The wiindigoo pushed through the wounded children, a wicked storm over their heads, with the robots close behind; the robots repeated parts of his promises to devour the children. The innocent victims were amused by the strange sentences. The cannibal settled on the dark side, his back to the sea, and the wild blue lights on the ships in the distance.

"This is your last chance," croaked Truman.

"Nothing has ever been my last," said the wiindigoo.

"You have the last choice," said Stone.

"Should the coin be there, the heirs lose, and the children are mine," said the wiindigoo. He smiled in the shadows and soughed to the hushed children; the low sounds of his voice touched the children with loneliness.

Panda was told to remain with the children and remember their stories of the moccasin game. The other robots were cued to the directions of the cannibal, his cold manner and incisive tone.

Miigis and Blue Ishi taunted the wiindigoo with blue spirit catchers and bear paw banners. The children behind the cannibal shivered and began to dance in circles to stay warm.

"Choose one of the four moccasins," said Stone.

"Felipa wore these," said the wiindigoo.

"Yes, she wore the pair on the right," said Stone.

"Which one would you chose?" asked the cannibal. He watched the heirs for a sign, a curl of the lips, a turn of the eye, that would indicate the location of the marked coin. "There is no ice woman to protect you tonight."

"Felipa wore a hole in one moccasin, you could choose that one and lose the world, and now you wonder what my gesture means," said Stone. The heirs hummed, the manicurists pounded a water drum, and a tribal rattle sounded in the hemlocks.

The wiindigoo touched each blue moccasin with a stick; he watched the heirs, but each time the responses were different. When he touched the fourth moccasin, the one with the coin and the war herb, the heirs and children were silent, as if their lives were in suspension. A mongrel moaned and the children laughed. The wiindigoo was convinced by the mongrel and was about to reach for the fourth moccasin when he was warned to hold back his choice.

"Wait, as you choose a moccasin you should know that the marked coin has been placed with a dangerous war herb," said Stone.

"Not even a robot would believe that," said the wiindigoo.

"Not even a robot," said a robot.

"You lose with the war herb," said Stone.

"So much concentration on this last moccasin," said the wiindigoo. "So, you must have thought the one with the hole would be too obvious."

"Fools choose the obvious," said Luckie. She had been in the shadows, concerned that she not tease or distract the cannibal from the game, but she could not hold back.

"The obvious trickster is the loser," said the wiindigoo.

"Tribal worlds would end," said Stone.

"The last chance is over the end," said the wiindigoo.

"Carp Radio would like you to tell our listeners about the game, what goes into a decision to end the world," said Luckie. She pushed a microphone close to his mouth and pretended they were on the air. "Admiral White lives with the most dangerous man in the world, the man who could end the night and talk radio with the drop of a blue moccasin." The wiindigoo turned to the side and remained silent in the shadow of the statue. No one had ever heard his voice on radio; the heirs wondered if his evil voice could even be recorded.

"The war herb would end the tribe, the heirs, the children, the nation, the world you are so eager to devour," warned Stone. "You would be here alone with the robots."

"The last gambit of the heirs," said the wiindigoo.

"The war herb would terminate the world, a bioactivated evanescence, only you and the robots would survive, and you would be mocked by the robots forever," said Stone.

"Your best diversion," said the wiindigoo.

"Who would you be without the heirs and the children to menace?" asked Stone. He brushed each of the moccasins and the children chanted, "wiindigoo, wiindigoo," louder and louder with each moccasin.

The wiindigoo leaned closer to the game and reached out to touch the last moccasin. "Would you be gone with this moccasin?"

"Your choice could be your last moccasin game, nothing would remain if you reveal the war herb, nothing more human than the robots, and our memories in the stone, but even a demon needs humans," said Stone.

The heirs and children were silent; the scientists were overcome, and the wiindigoo paused close to the four blue moccasins. At the instant he was about to choose a moccasin, the sky came alive with laser figures.

Almost Browne created a host of laser figures, the most momentous of his time, in the clear night sky on both sides of the moccasin game near the Trickster of Liberty.

Jesus Christ and Christopher Columbus arose in the south and walked to the moccasin game near the statue, a return visit from their earlier appearance in the sky over the stone tavern near the headwaters.

Crazy Horse, Black Elk, and Louis Riel were eminent laser figures in the north; they wore brilliant moccasins; they waited with the other figures in the night sky near the statue.

Felipa Flowers and Pocahontas arose in the east with a burst of light over Boundary Bay. Admire whistled, the mongrels barked, the heirs and children shouted to the morning stars to come home. The other figures turned and saluted as the two women walked toward the statue. The seven figures danced around the Trickster of Liberty and then disappeared at the end of the Miigis Marina.

"The soldier weed would end your game forever," said Stone.

"The game never ends," said the wiindigoo. He paused over the blue moccasins, raised his hand, and then moved back into the shadows. The mere mention of the soldier weed caused the cannibal to reconsider his choice of moccasins.

The wiindigoo had no interest in planets or the morning star, but he was pleased with the robots, the laser dancers in the night sky, and the soldier weed games at Point Assinika.

Admire whistled a tune from the *New World* Symphony by Antonín Dvořák. The children danced on the marina, and their wounds were healed once more in a moccasin game with demons.

EPILOGUE

Christopher Columbus landed in the New World with a striven western gaze that would be overturned in five centuries by the tribal people he saw as naked servants with no religion. "Our Lord pleasing, I will carry off six of them at my departure to Your Highnesses, in order that they may learn to speak," he wrote in his journal. The record of his first stare inscribed the end of peace on the islands and the source of loneliness in the New World.

The concise description of the island tribes as naked, with no "clothes, no arms, no possessions, no iron, and now no religion," was the birth of slavery and crude anthropology in the New World, wrote Kirkpatrick Sale in *The Conquest of Paradise: Christopher Columbus and the Columbian Legacy*.

Cristóbal Colón, Colombo, Colom, Colomb, or Columbus, has "given his name to more geographic places than any other actual figure in the history of the world, with the exception only of Queen Victoria; in the United States he surpasses all other eponyms except Washington," according to Sale.

Columbus and his civilization would discover no salvation in the New World. The missions, exploitations, racial vengeance, and colonialization ended the praise of deliverance; the conquistadors buried the tribal healers and their stories in the blood.

184

The consciousness of nurturance was there in tribal cultures, but the West has "tried for five centuries to resist the simple truth," wrote Sale. "We resist it further only at risk of the imperilment—worse, the likely destruction—of the earth."

Columbus arises in tribal stories that heal with humor the world he wounded; he is loathed, but he is not a separation in tribal consciousness. The Admiral of the Ocean Sea is a trickster overturned in his own stories five centuries later.

"The novel is born not of the theoretical spirit, but of the spirit of humor," wrote Milan Kundera in *The Art of the Novel*. "A character is not a simulation of a living being. It is an imaginary being. . . . The novel is the imaginary paradise of individuals. It is the territory where no one possesses the truth."

Christopher Columbus is quoted from translations of his journals that were published in *Admiral of the Ocean Sea: A Life of Christopher Columbus*, and *The Great Explorers*, by Samuel Eliot Morison; *The Log of Christopher Columbus*, translated by Robert Fuson; *Christopher Columbus: The Dream and Obsession*, by Gianni Granzotto; *The Four Voyages of Christopher Columbus*, by J. M. Cohen; and *The Journal of Christopher Columbus*, translated by Cecil Jane.

Columbus was an originator of New World "descriptions and narration," and on his "texts rests the pile of later literature," wrote Mary Campbell in *The Witness and the Other World*. Columbus "intersects both the political history that enlarged and demythologized the world of the traveler and the literary history of the travel account." He was a "crucial enabling agent of history."

The author considered other sources on exploration and colonial discourse: *Columbus, Cortés, and Other Essays*, by Ramón Iglesia; *Discoverers, Explorers, Settlers*, by Wayne Franklin; *Image of the New World*, by Gordon Brotherston; and *Colonial Encounters*, by Peter Hulme.

"Columbus sailed from Palos, Andalusia, on August third, with three ships manned by a total company of about ninety, among whom were at least six Jews," wrote Seymour Liebman in *The Jews in New Spain.* Columbus had no monk or priest with him on the first voyage, "in a time when no venture was undertaken without the presence of a representative of the Church." Kirkpatrick Sale argues that the evidence to support the idea that Columbus was a Jew is circumstantial and "there is no reason to give it credence." Robert Fuson, on the other hand, wrote that there is evidence that he was of "Jewish background, at least on one side of his family. Salvador de Madariaga and Simon Wiesenthal have provided more than enough documentation to convince any objective person. This does not mean that Columbus was anything less than a devout Christian; on that point the Log itself gives eloquent testimony. But a convert, or the descendant of a convert, did not boast of Jewish ancestry in 15th century Spain."

The author has made use of names and information on Sephardic Jews from *The Sephardim of England*, by Albert Hyamson, an outstanding history of the Spanish and Portuguese Jewish communities; and *The Secret Mission of Christopher Columbus*, by Simon Wiesenthal.

"A few months before Columbus's voyage in 1492, Spain enacted the Edict of Expulsion, compelling Jews to leave or convert to Catholicism under threat of death," the *New York Times* reported on November 11, 1990. Some of these Sephardic Jews who converted to Catholicism have "found refuge and obscurity in the mountains of New Mexico.

"Although most of these early colonizers lived as practicing Catholics, a significant number, often called 'conversos,' continued to cling secretly to Jewish traditions, lighting candles on Fridays, reciting Hebrew prayers, circumcising baby boys, baking unleavened bread, keeping the Sabbath." These traditions have survived over five centuries.

Louis Riel was imagined from *Louis Riel: The Rebel and the Hero*, by Hartwell Bowsfield; *Strange Empire*, by Joseph Kinsey Howard; and *The Trial of Louis Riel*, by John Coulter.

John Smith may have imagined the "peril from which Pocahontas supposedly saved him," wrote Helen Rountree in *Pocahontas's People*. She "is made to shine as an exception to the 'savagery' around her and depicted as a heroine who 'saved' the

English colony. . . ." The rescue of Smith "has been taken by some historians to be a formal adoption procedure." Other sources are *Pocahontas and Her World*, by Philip Barbour; *Pocahontas*, by Grace Steele Woodward; and *Indians Abroad*, by Carolyn Thomas Foreman.

James Fenimore Cooper wrote in the preface to his novel *Mercedes of Castile*, published in 1840, that everyone knows "Columbus had seamen in his vessels, and that he brought some of the natives of the islands he had discovered, back with him to Spain. The reader is now made much more intimately acquainted with certain of these individuals, we will venture to say, than he can be possibly by the perusal of any work previously written." His novel was one of nine that had been published in four centuries.

Antonin Dvořák was director of the Conservatory of Music in New York City at the time he composed his *New World* Symphony for the 1893 Columbian Exposition in Chicago. The exposition had been postponed to raise more money to complete the buildings.

President Grover Cleveland touched the gold and ivory telegraph key that started the machines of the exposition and the adoration of the explorer: millions of school children pledged their allegiance to the flag on cue for the first time; Frederick Jackson Turner presented his frontier thesis that summer to the American Historical Association; and the government issued a memorial coin on the quadricentennial with an image of Columbus on one side and "the *Santa María* on the reverse."

"The Native Americans who participated in the exhibits did not benefit from the exposition. Rather, they were the victims of a torrent of abuse and ridicule," wrote Robert Rydell in *All the World's a Fair*. "With Wounded Knee only three years removed, the Indians were regarded as apocalyptic threats to the values embodied in the White City who had to be tamed—an idea already captured and put into effect in Wild Bill's Congress of Rough Riders," which was performing several blocks from the fair.

Sale observed that the "whole event was an undertaking of superlatives," and the "past hundred years have not done much to change the position of Christopher Columbus as an American symbol—he is still the hero of scores of plays and operas and novels and poems, just as mythic as ever—but they have for the first time seen serious efforts to reassess his reputation in the light of the vast collection of new or previously unexamined documents."

Other publications the author considered include *The Vanished Library*, by Luciano Canfora; *The Ancient Maya*, by Sylvanus Morley, George Brainerd, and revised by Robert Sharer; *Time and the Highland Maya*, by Barbara Tedlock; *A Dream of Maya*, by Augustus and Alice Le Plongeon; *Maya*, by Charles Gallenkamp; *Mayan Dream Walk*, by Richard Luxton with Pablo Balam; *Collecting Rare Books*, by Jack Matthews; *Science Encounters the Indian*, by Robert Bieder; *Interpreting the Indian*, by Michael Castro; *Chippewa Customs*, by Frances Densmore; *History of the Ojibway Nation*, by William Warren; and "The Naming of America," by William Niederland, in *The Unconscious Today*, edited by Mark Kanzer.

"When we say that Columbus discovered America, we are summarizing the outcome of an extended period of claims and definitions, and we are opting for a particular outcome sanctioned at a particular time by a particular social agency," wrote Steve Woolgar in *Science: The Very Idea*. The sense of discovery is mediated by social conditions, as a "process rather than a point occurrence in time," and "the discovery process extends in time both before and after the initial announcement or claim."

The author quoted from *Making Sex: Body and Gender from the Greeks to Freud*, by Thomas Laqueur, and made use of other publications on science and genetics: *The Search for Eve*, by Michael Brown; *Mind Children: The Future of Robot and Human Intelligence*, by Hans Moravec; *The New Biology*, by Robert Augros and George Stanciu; *The Blind Watchmaker*, by Richard Dawkins; *Gene Wars*, by Charles Piller and Keith Yamamoto; and *The Redundant Male*, by Jeremy Cherfas and John Gribbin.

The Dominican Republic commissioned an enormous monument to celebrate the quincentenary of Christopher Columbus. The *El Faro a Colón* "is equipped with lights that can project the shape of a cross high into the clouds" over the slums of Santa Domingo, reported the *Sunday Times* of London.

"Despite criticism that such extravagance is incompatible with the country's grim economic predicament," the blind, octogenarian president Joaquin Balaguer said, "the people need shoes but they also need a tie." The tie to the great explorer and his search for gold has been a curse rather than a source of material salvation.

The mausoleum, where the partial remains of Columbus would be placed, is "billed as the brightest light in the Americas." About a hundred and fifty spotlights "will project the cross into the sky. This may seem ambitious in a country where power cuts of up to eight hours a day are common." The Dominican architect said, "We've got our own generator just in case."

Columbus is resented by the poor, "not least because in many Latin American countries his name is synonymous with the import of measles, typhus, yellow fever, and smallpox."

President Ronald Reagan paid tribute to Christopher Columbus as a "dreamer, a man of vision and courage, a man filled with hope for the future," as only he could understand. "Put it all together and you might say that Columbus was the inventor of the American Dream."

Christopher Columbus, no doubt, would rather be remembered as an obscure healer in the humor of a novel and crossblood stories than the simulated quiver in national politics; he deserves both strategies of survival in a wild consumer culture.

"I hope to Our Lord that it will be the greatest honor for Christianity, although it has been accomplished with such ease," he wrote at the end of his journal.

UNIVERSITY PRESS OF NEW ENGLAND publishes books under its own im-
print and is the publisher for Brandeis University Press, Brown University
Press, Clark University Press, University of Connecticut, Dartmouth College, Middlebury College Press, University of New Hampshire, University
of Rhode Island, Tufts University, University of Vermont, and Wesleyan
University Press.

Library of Congress Cataloging-in-Publication Data
Vizenor, Gerald Robert, 1934–
The heirs of Columbus / Gerald Vizenor.
p.   cm.
ISBN 0-8195-5241-0 (cl).—ISBN 0-8195-6249-1 (pa)
1. Indians of North America—Fiction. I. Title.
PS3572.I9H45   1991
813'.54 — dc20   91-8242

♾